PRAISE FOR LJ ROSS

What newspapers say

"She keeps company with the best mystery writers" – *The Times*

"LJ Ross is the queen of Kindle" – *Sunday Telegraph*

"Holy Island is a blockbuster" – *Daily Express*

"A literary phenomenon" – *Evening Chronicle*

"A pacey, enthralling read" – *Independent*

What readers say

"I couldn't put it down. I think the full series will cause a divorce, but it will be worth it."

"I gave this book 5 stars because there's no option for 100."

"Thank you, LJ Ross, for the best two hours of my life."

"This book has more twists than a demented corkscrew."

"Another masterpiece in the series. The DCI Ryan mysteries are superb, with very realistic characters and wonderful plots. They are a joy to read!"

THE BAY

A SUMMER SUSPENSE MYSTERY

BOOKS BY LJ ROSS

THE ALEXANDER GREGORY THRILLERS:

1. *Impostor*
2. *Hysteria*
3. *Bedlam*
4. *Mania*

THE DCI RYAN MYSTERIES:

1. *Holy Island*
2. *Sycamore Gap*
3. *Heavenfield*
4. *Angel*
5. *High Force*
6. *Cragside*
7. *Dark Skies*
8. *Seven Bridges*
9. *The Hermitage*
10. *Longstone*
11. *The Infirmary (Prequel)*
12. *The Moor*
13. *Penshaw*
14. *Borderlands*
15. *Ryan's Christmas*
16. *The Shrine*
17. *Cuthbert's Way*
18. *The Rock*
19. *Bamburgh*
20. *Lady's Well*

THE SUMMER SUSPENSE MYSTERIES:

1. *The Cove*
2. *The Creek*
3. *The Bay*

THE BAY

A SUMMER SUSPENSE MYSTERY

LJ ROSS

ISBN: 978-1-912310-83-8

First published in September 2023 by Dark Skies Publishing

Cover layout by Stuart Bache

Cover artwork by Andrew Davidson

Typeset by Riverside Publishing Solutions Limited

"The gods visit the sins of the fathers upon the children."

— Euripides

PROLOGUE

Tyneside, mid-1990s

They came to take her father away in the early hours of Sophie's fourth birthday.

She awoke to the sound of hard banging on the front door, followed by the angry shouts of police officers as they burst inside, splintering the wood from its hinges. Clutching her favourite stuffed toy, which happened to be a pink rabbit by the name of 'Flopsy', Sophie wriggled out of bed and crept towards the sliver of light shining beneath her bedroom door.

Had Uncle Terry come to visit again?

He wasn't her *real* uncle, but a friend of her father's, so she called him 'Uncle'. He was very loud and smelled funny; like the carpet on the floor of the pub where they went for a carvery lunch on Sundays.

But it wasn't Uncle Terry, because she couldn't hear anybody laughing at his silly jokes, or telling him to, 'Get himself away home before he woke up the whole estate.' Instead, she heard a stream of bad words she knew she wasn't supposed to repeat, followed by her mother's tearful cries.

What's all this about?

What's going on?

She heard crashing and banging in the kitchen, and her legs began to shake. Paralysed by fear but too frightened to stay still, she tiptoed onto the landing and peered through the stair rails to the hallway below. Beneath the garish light of her mother's crystal chandelier, she saw her parents held off to one side by two men in uniform, whose faces were as hard as the protective helmets they wore.

Another officer joined them, and spoke in undertones.

"Found a big wad of cash in the kitchen, Guv—"

"*What*?" Her mother turned to her father in confusion. "There isn't any money in the house— tell them, Mick!"

When he said nothing, and continued to stare at a spot on the wall above her head, she began to cry.

"My daughter's asleep upstairs," she implored them, scrubbing tears from her eyes. "*Please*— she'll be worried about all the noise—"

"They didn't tell us there was a kid," one of the officers muttered. "Better call child services."

They turned back to the woman.

"She'll be taken into care, while you're both detained."

"*No!*"

The word burst from Sophie's mouth, and they looked up in surprise to see a pretty, dark-haired child watching them with big, terrified eyes from the landing above.

"Sweetheart! Don't—don't worry—" her mother started to say, but tears ran in rivulets down her face, clogging her throat.

One of the officers held her mother back while another started up the stairs and, to Sophie's eyes, he was a monster dressed all in black, the stuff of nightmares.

She began to scream.

You're scaring her! Please—

"Daddy!"

Daddy!

To her shame, a trickle crept down her leg, wetting her best Little Mermaid nightie.

"Come on, pet, we'll get you a packet of crisps or something," the officer said, and plucked her from the floor where she cowered, a tiny ball of shaking skin and bone.

As they carried her away from her home and family, the last thing Sophie remembered was not her mother's ravaged face, nor the balloons they'd put up in the living room for her to find later that morning alongside Barbie's Malibu Dream House.

It wasn't the sight of their neighbours watching from doorways and upstairs windows, nor the stench of body odour and urine drenching her young skin.

It was her father's silence throughout the ordeal, and the knowledge that he never so much as looked at her before she was taken away by strangers.

That, she would never forget.

Six weeks later

"We can't go away without Daddy."

Sophie's plaintive voice was almost her mother's undoing.

"Please," she whispered, swiping away fresh tears. "Try to understand. Your daddy can't come with us. He's—he's gone away."

"Where?"

Her mother didn't answer, but remained standing at the kitchen window smoking the last of her packet of Marlborough Lights while she waited for an unmarked police car to arrive.

It hadn't taken long for word to spread.

Mick Gallagher finally got his comeuppance, they said around the doors.

Not before time.

Everybody had known about Mick Gallagher— the *real* Mick Gallagher—except his wife and child.

It had taken six weeks before the courts deemed it safe for Sophie to be returned home to her mother, who'd been released without charge after long hours inside an interrogation room. But, when Sophie leapt from the social worker's car, she found very little remained of the home she'd once known. The front of their house had been defaced by graffiti; spray-painted words she couldn't read but knew, somehow, were very bad. When the new, makeshift front door swung open it revealed her mother, a woman of twenty-four, whose face was shadowed by all that had come to light in the intervening weeks and whose eyes seemed decades older than before. They wore a distant, faraway expression she was too young to understand as being a by-product of strong anti-depressants, and her arms were thin and wiry as they held her in a tight embrace.

Now, a few days later, her mother's eyes wore the same unfocused expression as they stared listlessly out the window.

Sophie sat down on the linoleum and cradled Flopsy, who remained by her side as a constant companion.

"Time to go," her mother said, a few minutes later.

"I don't want to—"

Kim Gallagher could barely process her own shock at finding out the extent of her husband's crimes, let alone form the words to explain it to a child of four.

"Do as you're told," she said softly.

When the little girl began to cry again—big, rolling tears that made her hiccup—Kim found the strength to sit cross-legged on the floor beside her.

"It's a beautiful place, where we're going," she said, and tried to sound excited. "It has a golden, sandy beach with lots of shells to collect, and—and, there's ice cream shops and an arcade, I think. There's lots of boats, just like there is here. There'll be other children to play with, and you'll be starting school in September, so you'll make lots of nice new friends."

Sophie heard the forced note of cheer, and looked up into her mother's desperate eyes.

"I thought it was just a holiday!"

Kim shook her head. "No, sweetheart. We're starting a new life. It'll be exciting—"

"Why can't I go to school *here*? Emily's going to St Joseph's—"

Kim thought of the words Emily's mother, her former friend, had thrown at her the previous week. "I'll tell you about it when you're older," she said.

There came a loud bang on the door which made Sophie jump, her eyes wide with remembered fear.

Kim held out her arms so the little girl could crawl onto her lap, and decided to let them wait.

"What's it called—the place we're going to?" Sophie said, after a moment's silence.

"Cornwall," her mother replied. "A place called St Ives."

"Will Daddy be able to find us there? I don't want him to get lost."

Kim closed her eyes briefly, a single tear rolling down her cheek as she held Sophie tightly against her chest.

"He's already lost," she whispered.

CHAPTER 1

St Ives, Cornwall

Twenty-five years later

The sky was ablaze.

Detective Sergeant Sophie Keane thought this as she watched the sun set over the town of St Ives, leaving behind a dazzling canvas of pink and yellow as it prepared to fall off the edge of the world. The light in those parts had often been described as 'ethereal', something painters tried to capture time and again but, like a half-remembered dream, it evaded even the most talented of artists.

"Not bad, eh?"

"I've seen worse," she agreed, and turned away from the window to greet her friend.

Luke Malone was the owner of the beautiful new art gallery where they now stood, which had been built on the wharf overlooking the little harbour, and the sea beyond. It boasted panoramic views spanning the town to one side, with its picturesque collection of old stone fishing cottages, all the way towards Godrevy lighthouse on the other, half swathed in mist on the far horizon.

"How's the opening going?" she asked him.

Luke smiled across the open-plan space towards his wife, Gabrielle, who stood chatting with some of the more illustrious members of the local community, including the mayor and several town councillors. If he didn't know better, he'd have said she was bored witless, and made a mental note to thank her profusely—and thoroughly—as soon as they got home. With that pleasant thought circling his mind, he raised a hand to acknowledge his friend, Nick, who'd made the journey from Helford in support of his fiancée, Kate, whose illustrations formed part of the new exhibition of 'fresh talent' that evening. The remaining guests were a mix of local journalists and longstanding patrons of the arts, as well as the family and friends of the artists whose work hung in smart frames on the freshly-painted walls.

"It's going well," he said. "Kate was telling me she's been working on a project with a big children's author to illustrate a brand-new series of adventure books, and Gabi can hardly wait to get her hands on some of them for the bookshop."

He smiled, thinking of his wife's passion for books, and of the life they'd built together in Carnance, a cove on the other side of the peninsula.

"I'm glad things have turned out so well for Kate," Sophie said, thinking back to events the previous year. "She and Nick seem very happy together, and her son is cute as a button."

There was a note in her voice he might have described it as 'wistful'. Not envious, nor jealous; merely a sound that conveyed a longing for something she didn't yet have.

He wondered if she was aware of it herself.

"I'm sorry I don't have any more news about the theft of that painting," Sophie said, steering the conversation back to business. "We're still investigating—something's bound to turn up."

The previous day, one of the star pieces of Luke's exhibition had been stolen on the eve of the gallery's opening night, apparently without any witnesses to the fact.

"What I can't understand is why they took *that* painting in particular," he muttered. "Of course, *Moonlit Bay* was very good, I wouldn't have included it in the catalogue otherwise, but Dean Mostend is hardly a well-known artist. I can't imagine they'd be able to shift it for very much on the black market."

He referred to one of the new artists he'd hoped to showcase, whose enormous oil painting of St Ives Bay in stormy weather was striking and bold, and sure to appeal to a collector with an eye for an appreciating commodity.

"It's a shame Dean didn't come along this evening, but he probably can't face seeing the blank space on the wall where his painting should have been," he added. "There's been a lot of interest in it—and him—so we might have been able to reel in a few private commissions, if nothing else."

Sophie flicked through the catalogue she held in her hand, to refresh her memory.

Moonlit Bay was, as Luke had said, a striking piece of original art, depicting a group of fishermen unloading barrels from a boat late at night, their bodies illuminated by the light of a full moon which shone an eerie white light across the rippling tide which lashed against the boat's stern and crashed in foaming waves against the harbour wall.

"It's hardly something that could fit in your back pocket," she said, noting its dimensions.

"Somebody *must* have seen something, but it's been less than twenty-four hours. We're still continuing with door-to-door interviews, which could throw something up."

"D'you think it might have been kids?" Luke asked, thinking of the small but persistent band of teens who liked to joyride or lift the odd trinket here and there, usually to assuage boredom or sell in exchange for drugs.

Sophie frowned, then shook her head. "I wondered that myself, but whoever took the painting knew how to get around the alarm system," she pointed out. "This wasn't a 'smash and grab' affair, which is something I'd expect from our usual merry band of idiots."

He grinned at that, before his face fell back into serious lines. "So you think we're looking for a professional?"

"Possibly," is all she would say.

Luke noted the raised hand of a potential buyer. "Let me know if you catch any leads in the coming days," he said. "I've got to go and schmooze someone into buying a piece of modernist art. In the meantime, try to enjoy yourself and have another glass of champagne. You're off-duty, and hey, you never know, some handsome stranger might wander in and sweep you off your feet with talk of Picasso and Barbara Hepworth."

Sophie laughed, shook her head, then turned back to the window to watch the sky turn from pink to mauve. Luke meant well, she was sure, but the last thing she needed was a man in her life—or anyone, for that matter. She knew the emotional cost of loving, and the inevitable heartbreak when they left or let you down. Giving her heart into another person's safekeeping wasn't a mistake she planned on making ever again.

After a few minutes passed, she sensed a presence beside her.

"Couldn't seal the deal?" she asked, and turned with a ready smile in place, expecting to find her friend had returned. Except, to her surprise, it was not Luke but rather a man she'd never seen in her life before. Tall, black-haired and possessed of a startling pair of blue eyes, her body responded immediately to the very embodiment of 'Tall, Dark and Handsome', and her first thought was to feel irrationally angry about it.

"Not just yet," he replied, with a slow smile.

"What?"

"The deal," he reminded her. "Whatever it is, I haven't sealed it yet."

To her horror, she felt a blush creep over her skin.

He stepped closer to the window, an action which brought them shoulder to shoulder.

"It's a pretty night, isn't it?" he said. "I think there's a storm brewing, though."

Sophie followed the direction of his gaze and saw only clear skies overhead and calm waters lapping against the shoreline.

"What makes you say that?"

"Just a feeling," he said, and then leaned down, so she felt the warmth of his breath beside her right ear. "That, and the shipping forecast."

He straightened again, and flashed a smile that was devastating.

"Um—" she said, and cast around for something more intelligent to say. "Are you one of the artists being exhibited this evening?"

He shook his head. "Just an interested party," he said, turning back to the view. "I remember this old building from a long time ago—before it was a gallery."

As a rule, she couldn't stand evasiveness, so that was an automatic strike against him—no matter how blue his eyes might have been.

"Oh? You used to live around here?"

He nodded. "In another lifetime," he said, irritating her again. "I'm visiting the area for old time's sake. What about you? Are you one of the artists?"

"Maybe in another lifetime," she parroted, and then reached inside the pocket of her smart cream trousers to retrieve her warrant card. "DS Sophie Keane, Devon and Cornwall Police."

His blue eyes flicked over the card, then back up to her face.

"Even better," he said. "Now I know who to come to, if I should stumble across a body."

Before she could formulate an appropriate response, he leaned in again to whisper a parting thought.

"Next time, I hope to see you in your uniform, Detective Sergeant Keane."

He had the audacity to wink at her before strolling off into the crowd, his dark head mingling with others until he disappeared from sight.

It was only after the flames of outrage had cooled to disdain that she realised he hadn't told her his name, nor anything else about himself.

Sophie had all manner of police resources at her disposal, but the fastest way to gather information in a town like St Ives was to seek out one of a small number of knowledgeable sources, any of whom could be relied upon to supply her with hot gossip about the people in their local community.

Her first port of call was Jenna Pearce, her boss's wife.

"Mrs Pearce," Sophie greeted her, with just a touch of deference.

"Sophie, dear, you know I've told you to call me Jenna," the other woman said, but they both knew that day would never come.

There were ways of doing things in that part of the world. Conventions that must be followed to keep the peace, which would be harder to maintain without the cooperation of women like Jenna Pearce and her circle of friends. Considering the cost-benefit ratio, Sophie had come to the sensible conclusion that it was worth biting her lip and sacrificing a modicum of self-respect for the benefit of the greater good.

That didn't mean she enjoyed it.

She gestured to the art on the walls around them. "Have you seen anything you like?"

They exchanged pleasantries for a few minutes, until Sophie deemed it an appropriate moment to ask the question uppermost in her mind.

Predictably, Jenna was already one step ahead. "I bet you're wondering who that young man is," she said, in a stage whisper that turned heads and grated on Sophie's nerves. "Now, *there's* something I wouldn't mind taking home!"

She let out a bawdy laugh through lips coated in three shades of pink lipstick, which she licked in anticipation of sharing a fresh round of gossip.

"His name's *Gabriel Rowe* and he's staying at Wharf House—you know, that lovely old house on the far side, before you get to the pier?"

Sophie nodded, for it was one of the most beautiful buildings in town, painted a delicate pastel pink, with trailing ivy over its old stone walls and other creepers that bloomed throughout the year. It had been built flush to the harbour, so that its outer wall merged with the harbour wall and afforded its owner direct access onto the sand, which became a larger beach when the tide went out. It was a lovely spot, and a perfect home for any family.

"He's renting it?" she asked.

"*No*," Jenna said, drawing out the word for dramatic effect. "Gabriel is the owner. I thought he'd sold the place years ago, but apparently not. His family used to rent it out for years, after the accident—"

She paused, clucked her tongue, and waited.

"What accident?" Sophie asked, obligingly.

"Well, you know, it was a terrible thing," Jenna rattled on. "His father, John, was the local doctor for *years* but then, after Gabriel's mother passed away—cervical cancer, you know, poor soul—he went off the rails. Started drinking."

Jenna made a crass motion with her hand, as if the words were not enough for Sophie to understand their meaning, and her eyes strayed across the room to seek Gabriel out, concerned in case he should happen to see it.

"All of this was before your time," Jenna was saying. "You came to live here—when was it, dear?"

"I was four," Sophie said, though she was quite sure Jenna remembered. "I'm twenty-nine, now."

"Doesn't time just *fly*," the woman exclaimed, and took a long glug from her champagne flute before continuing. "Well now, where was I? This must have happened a couple of years before you moved here, and Gabriel couldn't have been more than nine or ten at the time ..."

Which made him seven or eight years older than herself, came the unbidden thought.

"You were telling me about his father being the local doctor," she said.

"Yes, of course I was. Well, John hit the bottle, and that can't have been easy for poor Gabriel. I used to see him pottering about on the sand by himself, many a time, and of course we had him over for tea with Cameron quite often. They were in the same year at school, you know, and I was a great friend of his mother, Eleanor—God rest her."

Jenna heaved a sigh, and her chest puffed out, straining the buttons on the tight satin blouse she wore.

"It all came to a head, late one night. John must've been *steaming* drunk, because he left

Gabriel asleep in his bed, wandered out of the house and along the pier...well, you know how the tide can be. He fell, and the waves battered him against the rocks. Dreadful, just dreadful. And, to think, little Gabriel woke up the next morning to find himself all alone. The poor lamb."

Sophie took a moment before speaking to ensure her voice remained steady and professional, but all she could see was a raven-haired little boy who'd lost his mother and then his father, all before his eleventh birthday. To lose one parent was bad enough, but both...

"What happened to Gabriel after his father died? Did he have anyone to care for him?"

Unexpectedly, she caught sight of him, standing on the far side of the room chatting with Nick and Kate. As if sensing her appraisal, he turned to look at her, blue eyes clashing with brown, and it was as though he'd reached across the room and touched her.

She looked away, feeling unsettled.

"His mother's sister took him in—they live in Truro," Jenna said. "I'd have thought they would've sold the house, to help out with expenses…well, there you have it. Gabriel's been gone for nearly thirty years, and nobody around here seems to know what he's been doing with himself in all that time—though, by the looks of him, he's done well enough."

There was a gleam in her eye that seemed to suggest she would be making it her business to find out more and, had Sophie not been wary of conveying any personal feeling on the matter, she might have been moved to tell her to leave the poor man alone. Besides, digging into people's backgrounds was *her* job.

Her eyes strayed back across the room but, this time, he was nowhere in sight.

Sophie told herself it was professional curiosity and not disappointment that caused the sinking feeling in her stomach.

Later, when she was finally able to extricate herself from Jenna Pearce's fulsome company,

Sophie made her farewells and stepped out into the balmy summer night, only to feel the first patter of rain fall against her upturned skin.

As Gabriel had predicted, a storm was coming.

CHAPTER 2

The storm raged all through the night, battering against the exposed walls of the town and howling like a drunken sailor through its cobbled streets. Rain lashed against windowpanes and rooftops, keeping awake all but the most longstanding residents of St Ives, who understood the deluge would pass just as quickly as it had come. Sophie might have counted herself amongst their number, and it was not the rain that kept her awake but thoughts of a lonely little boy who was now a grown man, forced to leave all he'd known to begin a new life elsewhere.

It was something she was uniquely qualified to understand.

Snatched memories from long ago haunted her until dawn, rising to the surface of her mind like spectres, tormenting her with images she'd spent more than twenty years trying to forget. She chose not to remember the man who'd fathered her, nor of the times he'd been kind to her before they discovered the truth about the person he really was. She and her mother had begun a new life, with new names, and they'd never spoken the truth to anyone.

Not then, not now...not ever.

It was no great leap to understand why she'd chosen to enter the police service; it gave her a feeling of solace to know that her daily work went some way to balancing the scales of rights and wrongs in the world. She told herself that, for every person her father had ever hurt, she would prevent other families from suffering a similar fate by working hard each day to uphold law and order. It was a constant sweeping of the tide, she knew, but it gave her a sense of purpose and the comfort of knowing that she was nothing like *him*.

Consequently, she was already wide awake and sipping her third coffee of the morning when her mobile phone began to shrill.

"Keane."

"Sarge, it's Turner."

She rolled her eyes, thinking of the young police constable she was training up for the detective's pathway. He had a good heart, and was eager to learn, but if she was in a less charitable frame of mind she might've said he wasn't the brightest bulb in the box.

Then again, raw intelligence wasn't everything.

Instinct, hard work, a steady pair of hands... they were just as important, and sometimes more so, in their line of work.

"What's up, Alex?"

"Sorry to call so early," he said, in a rush of words. "A call came through to the desk, just now..."

He trailed off, apparently waiting for some kind of response.

"Well?" she demanded. "Spit it out, before we both die of old age."

"It's—there's—um, there's a *body*, washed up on Porthgwidden beach. A dog-walker found it and called it straight in."

Sophie had thought he might've been calling to tell her that the missing painting had been found abandoned in a car park somewhere, or that a group of tourists had been involved in another brawl with the locals outside one of the pubs. Despite all the visitors who flocked to St Ives each year, they were lucky to have an extremely low body count, with most people dying through accidental or natural causes, so the fact that a body had turned up was the last thing she'd expected him to say.

She let out the breath she'd been holding in her chest, and her voice was calm when she spoke.

"Take another constable and get down to the scene to secure it. I'll call in forensics, but it'll take them a while to get across, depending on how busy the roads are—"

She paused to check the time on the large, wooden clock she'd fixed to her kitchen wall.

Six-fifteen.

"It's early, yet," she said. "But the weather's good, so people will be heading down to the beach soon. I want the body protected from the elements and prying eyes, so take the tent we keep in the basement at the station—you know the one I mean? That'll keep things private and protect the body from the worst of it until scenes of crime officers arrive."

Turner was nodding vigorously, until he remembered she couldn't see him through the telephone.

"Yes—of course—"

"And Turner? Don't go blabber-mouthing to all and sundry. We'll be saying nothing until next of kin are informed—that includes speaking to your brother at the local paper, is that understood?"

"Yes, guv," he said.

"I'll see you there—and, Alex? Bring a paper bag with you."

His sergeant ended the call before PC Turner could ask *why* he should bring a paper bag with him, but the reason became painfully obvious the moment he joined her in the easternmost corner of Porthgwidden beach a short time later, where a sheltered arc of powdery sand met the rocks. The beach itself was one of the smallest in St Ives, nestled between the main harbour and the slightly larger Porthmeor Beach, in the lee of an outcrop of headland known as 'The Island'. The land on either side blocked out most of the prevailing winds, making it a perfect spot for families with young children who were more interested in building sandcastles than surfboarding, and who could be easily sustained by a trip to the nearby beach café. However, thoughts of sausage rolls and pasties were far from Turner's mind as he trundled across the sand towards Sophie, dressed in a white polypropylene coverall while she stood as sentry beside the jumbled mass of sallow flesh that had once been a person.

"Oh—oh, God—"

Sophie turned sharply at his approach, and pointed towards the paper bag he'd folded and tucked in his trouser pocket.

"The bag, Turner. Use it—over there."

When he'd divested himself of the entire contents of his stomach and there was nothing left but bile, Turner cleaned himself up as best he could and made his way back across the sand towards his sergeant.

"Sorry—"

She handed him a bottle of chilled water, one of two she'd brought with her.

"Here, have some of this."

Never more grateful, he took the bottle and found that the act of drinking served as a useful distraction.

"How did you know I'd need it?"

"It's a punch to the belly, that first time," Sophie said, with a shrug. "I remember the first time I saw a DB. I threw up so hard I thought I was going to crack a rib."

He managed a smile, and sipped some more. "Does it get easier?"

"The throwing up?" she teased him. "Nah, still gives me one hell of a stitch. Why d'you think I'm holding my own water, Sherlock? Nobody's immune to this kind of horror—not even me."

She gave him another couple of minutes, until she spotted the arrival of two more constables in a squad car whom she'd drafted in from a nearby station to help with crowd management.

"Reinforcements have arrived," she said. "You think you can keep it together?"

Turner wasn't convinced, but nodded in a display of pure bravado. "I'm fine now."

Sophie wasn't convinced either, but gave him a bolstering nudge. "Good. Let's get that tent up, before forensics get here."

She turned to grab the pile of tarpaulin he'd dumped in the sand, then remembered.

"One last present for you, Turner," she said, retrieving a small blue bottle from her jacket pocket. "Dab a bit of this under your nose, and it'll help. Don't forget your coveralls and mask."

He caught the bottle in one hand, and looked down at the label.

Vicks.

It reminded him of childhood ailments and evenings spent at his grandmother's house, but menthol was far better than the cloying scent of death, so he applied a liberal dollop beneath his nostrils and breathed deeply.

"Ready?"

"Yeah. Let's see who he is."

"Was," she corrected him, softly. "It's only the shell we're dealing with now, Alex."

On which note, she turned away and prepared to face death.

CHAPTER 3

The shell Sophie had spoken of was so unrecognisable as to be unidentifiable, at least not by sight alone. The sea could be cruel, and this was never more so than in its treatment of the body that lay face-down in the sand, illuminated by the morning sun which burned away the sea fret and blazed its unforgiving light upon the cadaver's pale flesh. Naked and despoiled by fish, it was horribly bloated, the skin resembling that of a waxwork mannequin, marked and coarse after many hours at the mercy of the water and all that lay beneath it. Inside the claustrophobic confines of their makeshift tent, Sophie and her constable breathed hard between their teeth, expelling a faint but tangible scent that had begun to permeate the air as the temperature outside continued to rise and the body continued its natural process of putrefaction.

"Could've been a suicide," Turner suggested, from his position nearest the exit. "We might find a pile of clothes folded up somewhere with a note."

Sophie continued to study the body, and thought of how death was the last undignified action of the living.

"I don't think so," she said. "Look at his ankles."

"Do I have to?"

She gave Turner a hard stare.

"Okay, okay," he muttered, and forced himself to look down. "What am I looking for?"

"This," she said, and indicated a thick, dark line around each ankle, spreading to the lower calves. "It looks as though his ankles were bound together, maybe with rope, judging by the extent of abrasion to the skin. Any wear in that area would have attracted the attention of underwater scavengers, and decomposition would also be expedited. That's why his lower legs are in a worse state than the rest of him."

"How—" Turner swallowed bile, and moved back to the safety of the doorway, where he took a few deep breaths. "How do you know all that?"

"Experience," she said. "It doesn't look like suicide to me, especially factoring in the head trauma."

They both eyed a series of heavy gashes to the back of the man's head, one in particular having been forceful enough to split his skull.

"Might have hit some rocks after he drowned," Turner pointed out.

"We'll leave it to the experts," she decided and, as if on cue, they arrived at that very moment.

"DS Keane." The senior scenes of crimes officer dipped inside the tent, nodded cordially, then tutted towards the body. "Haven't had a floater in a little while, at least not around St Ives. Caught one the other week but that was over at Sennen— young surfer who was out of his depth."

There followed another *tut.*

The prosaic way in which he spoke of death annoyed her, but Sophie hadn't climbed the closed, predominantly male ranks of the Devon and Cornwall Police by snapping at every trifling annoyance. It was a hot-headed fool who burned bridges, and she knew the value of silence. Battles might have been won, but the war would be lost, so her mother used to say.

"Have you turned him over?"

"Not yet," she said, with a shake of her head. "We haven't touched anything."

The forensic specialist, whose name was Pete Irwin, made a rumbling sound of approval in his chest and proceeded to take pictures of the body from every conceivable angle. They watched him rustle this way and that until, the task complete, he straightened up and beckoned PC Turner forward with an imperious crook of his gloved finger.

"Give me a hand to flip him over, will you, lad?"

Turner looked as though he might pass out at the very thought, and Sophie took pity on him.

"Actually, I was about to ask PC Turner to take down a formal statement from the witness," she said. "I'll help you turn the body."

Irwin raised an eyebrow but didn't argue, and Turner escaped the stifling confines of the tent like a rat abandoning a sinking ship.

"Righty-o," Irwin said, cheerfully. "You're all gloved up? Good. I'll grab his torso, if you can manage the legs."

Sophie drew in a deep, fortifying breath through the face mask she wore, and braced herself.

"Ready."

On three, they turned him, and the man was laid bare to their professional gaze. In the seconds it took for her system to regulate itself, several things imprinted themselves on her mind's eye. The first was that someone had sliced away each of the man's fingertips and, upon closer inspection, she could see that his teeth had also been removed, leaving a hollowed, gaping jaw filled with ocean detritus. There were no other humanising features, the face having been almost entirely lost to the ravages of the sea, and she could only feel the deepest sympathy for whomever this man's family would turn out to be.

"Looks like a professional job," Irwin said, and raised his camera to continue the process of documenting the body. "Uh-oh, what have we here?"

Sophie had been lost in thought, racking her brain to think of any men between the ages of forty and sixty who'd been reported missing in the last few days. "What's that?"

Irwin was down on his haunches, brushing away the sand that caked itself to the uppermost layer of skin on the man's left forearm. "You'd better take a look at this."

She hurried over, and immediately wished she hadn't.

The breath lodged in her chest, and a primal scream echoed silently around the walls of her skull. There, carved into the dead man's skin, was a crude picture of a fish, the lines scored deep into his flesh so they might remain visible in spite of any interference—for a while, at least.

"What d' you make of—?"

Irwin's voice trailed off when he saw the sickly pallor of her skin, which had lost all trace of colour.

"I—it isn't possible—" she whispered, before stumbling out of the tent.

Black spots danced in front of her eyes as she weaved drunkenly across the sand, and Sophie felt herself falling.

"Sarge!"

Turner caught her as her legs began to crumple.

"Can't—can't breathe—"

PC Turner, who had not yet distinguished himself in any notable capacity, chose that moment to shine.

"Look at me, Sarge—Sophie," he said, nervously. "Just breathe in through your nose and out through your mouth. That's it," he said, nudging her into a seated position where she could lean forward and focus on taking air in and out of her body.

It worked, and her mind and body righted themselves, leaving her feeling embarrassed and humiliated in front of her staff.

She struggled upward. "I should—"

"Take a minute," Turner advised and, this time, he was the one to hold out a bottle of water. "Somebody once told me this helps."

She looked into his boyish face, and could have kissed him—if she wasn't already feeling so nauseated.

"Thank you."

He smiled. "All part of the service."

She took a long drink, and watched Irwin make his way towards her with a fatherly expression on his face, no doubt ready to dish out some misogynist advice about her being a little lady in the wrong business if she couldn't handle the sight of a dead body. Across the beach, a group of constables eyed her with open curiosity, surprised to see their sergeant displaying human frailty for the first time in living memory.

"I'll never hear the end of this," she muttered.

"Was it because you moved the body?" Turner asked, guiltily.

Sophie stood up again with a rustle of plastic. "No, it wasn't because of that," she said. "The body has a ritual marking in the shape of a fish, which looks to have been carved into the skin using a knife. I've seen that calling card before, a long time ago, and it gave me a shock because that particular killer is still behind bars, as far as I know."

"Who was it?" Turner asked.

"During his trial for murder, the media called him 'The Artist' because he left an intricately carved image of a fish on the body of his victim," she said. "He worked as a gangland enforcer, but liked to be creative where he could because it earned him a bigger street rep. He was convicted of one murder, but it's generally believed there are many more that are unaccounted for."

She looked out across the water, drawing strength from the silvery glint of sunlight touching the ocean, and her voice returned to normal.

"His name was Michael Gallagher," she said.

My father, she added silently.

CHAPTER 4

As soon as the formalities were complete and she'd overseen transferral of the body to the mortuary, Sophie left Turner and the other constables to complete their questioning of the local residents and business owners. She should have made her way directly to the police station, which was a blocky monstrosity around the back of the town's cinema. Instead, she left her car parked and walked the coastal pathway that wound its way from Porthgwidden around the headland and back towards the main harbour. She welcomed the sea air that buffeted her skin, drying the salty tears that had begun to fall, and kept walking, putting one foot in front of the other until she emerged through the back streets and out onto the wharf.

St Ives was awash with tourists at that time of year and, as the clock struck nine, they'd already begun to spill out of their holiday homes and hotels, joining the early-morning dog walkers on the beaches around the bay. Sophie was used to them, and understood their value to local hospitality and other businesses that relied on the influx of visitors with deep pockets in high season, but that morning she found their presence intolerable. She needed peace and quiet, the sound of the sea and the call of the gulls, and nothing more.

She moved to one of the benches overlooking the harbour and sank onto it, letting the morning breeze wash over her skin. After a few minutes spent watching the relentless tide, she took out her mobile phone and keyed in a number she knew by rote.

After a couple of rings, her call was answered.

"His Majesty's Prison Frankland. How may we help you today?"

"I—" The words caught on her tongue, but she forced them out. "My father is currently serving a life sentence for murder. His name is Michael Gallagher. I haven't chosen to remain in contact, but I wanted to know if he would be coming up for parole soon?"

"Do you have a reference number?"

Sophie recited the number, and heard a tap of keys at the other end of the line.

"Did you say you were family?"

"Yes."

"I don't have any record of family members listed here," the woman said.

"We were under witness protection," Sophie said, and rubbed at her temple, where a dull headache had begun to throb.

"Without any way of verifying that, I can't give out personal details about a prisoner."

Sophie contemplated using her police credentials to force the issue, then dismissed the idea. She'd held the new version of herself apart from her grubby past for too long to throw it all away for the sake of expediency.

Luckily, Fate stepped in to lend a hand.

"Come to think of it, there's already been a report in the local news, so I don't suppose there's anything wrong with me telling you that Michael Gallagher was released on compassionate grounds about two months ago," the woman said. "I'm surprised you weren't informed."

Sophie thought of the witness protection officer they'd been in regular contact with, during those first few years. They'd retired, to be replaced by another, who'd subsequently resigned to go and open a bakery. People moved on with their lives and, over time, the system forgot there was any need to worry about the family of a convicted killer.

"Do you have any idea where Gallagher might be, now?" she asked.

"I'm sorry, I don't know. Is there anything else I can help you with today?"

A hysterical laugh bubbled up in her throat, but she managed to contain it.

"No, that's all. Thank you."

Gabriel moved through the rooms of his house on the wharf, no longer furnished as it had been all those years ago but decorated in plain, nautical white. Curtains with small, embroidered anchors adorned the windows, and old, sepia-hued pictures of St Ives hung from the walls. All of this had been done by his aunt, and then a management company who had, for nearly thirty years, taken care of its upkeep. Consequently, when he stepped through the front door—now painted in a tasteful shade of beige that probably had some fancy name or another—he hadn't expected to feel any affinity to the house.

But he was wrong.

Beneath the strange furnishings and the floral scent of his cleaner's room diffuser, the walls remained the same and he was struck by the notion that they remembered everything, just as he did.

Come on, Gabe. Let's go fishing.

He spun around, seeking out his father's voice, but it was only a memory. As always, the disappointment was visceral.

"Am I going mad?" he'd asked a grief counsellor, once. "I'm hearing voices, for pity's sake."

"Not voices, plural. You hear *one* voice, your father's voice," she'd corrected him. "Your mind is processing grief. People often think they can smell a loved one's scent long after they've gone, or hear them speaking. Sometimes, they see strangers walking down the street who resemble the one who's passed, so they believe they've seen a ghost."

It had been a long time since Gabriel had experienced an auditory memory like that, and he was honest enough to admit it was deeply upsetting. However, it was also to be expected. This was his father's house and memories of him were woven into its very foundations, so it was hardly surprising his psyche should call up the memory of his voice.

Gabriel moved from the kitchen through to the living room, where he held a cup of coffee in his hand and gazed out of a picture window overlooking the bay. He smiled at a dog running on the beach, thought briefly that he'd go for a walk a bit later, then wandered to another window, which had been cut into the gable end of the house and faced inland towards the wharf. He watched people passing along the waterfront, some holding dogs on leads or marshalling children, until his gaze came to rest on the face of a woman seated on one of the wooden benches facing the harbour. She wore her dark brown hair in a mid-length style that was windblown and brushed back from her face, which was pale and marred by a look of extreme upset, but still arresting.

It was Detective Sergeant Keane.

He thought of the reason he'd come back to St Ives after so many years and decided it was a good time to go for that walk after all.

CHAPTER 5

"Penny for them."

Gabriel didn't wait to be invited, but settled himself on the bench beside Sophie and stretched out his long legs, crossing them at the ankles. In cotton shorts, a crisp white t-shirt and dark glasses, he was the very picture of relaxed coastal chic. She, on the other hand, was dressed in serviceable jeans with a washed-out linen shirt, added to which she was fairly certain she still carried an aroma of *death*, leftover from a morning spent manhandling a corpse.

At least he wasn't sitting downwind.

"My thoughts aren't even worth a penny," she said, and nodded towards the house a few hundred yards along the waterfront. "I hear you're staying at Wharf House? It's a lovely spot."

He smiled, without much mirth. "Word travels fast around here, doesn't it?"

Sophie crossed her legs, unconsciously mirroring his stance. "It sure does," she agreed. "Especially in certain circles."

When he made no further comment, she cleared her throat. "I was sorry to hear about your parents," she said. "It must be a strange homecoming for you."

They were words Gabriel had heard a hundred times before but, this time, they managed to hit a nerve. Unexpectedly, he felt his chest tighten, the old grief rising up again to rob him of speech.

Noticing his sudden intake of breath, she shifted towards him, compassion overtaking her natural reserve. "I'm sorry, I didn't mean to upset you—"

"You haven't," he said, keeping his voice level. "It's been thirty years since my father died, and even longer for my mother."

So long he barely remembered her.

"As I said yesterday, my childhood here in St Ives feels like it was another lifetime."

"Why did you come back?"

She was full of questions, he thought. "Nostalgia," he replied shortly. "I wanted to close the door to the past. As the rumour mill has no doubt already informed you, I'm thinking about selling the old place. There've been various offers over the years, but my aunt never felt right about letting go of the house where she and my father grew up as children. It was left to my father, who left it to me in his will. It's been in the family for generations."

Sophie watched the play of sunlight over his dark hair, and wished she could read the expression behind his eyes.

"I don't know why I haven't sold it already," he muttered, but that was a lie.

He knew why he hadn't sold it.

"You seemed lost in thought when I interrupted you," he said, changing the subject. "I heard about the stolen painting—I hope there hasn't been another theft?"

Sophie thought of the usual petty crime that happened the world over, even in a picturesque coastal town such as theirs, and shook her head.

"Nothing of that kind," she said. "Although, if you have anything valuable in the house, I'd take care to lock it away or use an alarm system."

Gabriel smiled. "It would feel sacrilegious. People always leave their front doors unlocked, or, at least, they did when I lived around here."

"They still do," she said, with a touch of professional pride.

In a town with a fluctuating, transient population, it was a difficult job to keep on top of the occasional gangs of thieves who roamed the county looking for easy pickings from unwary tourists, but she and her team made sure that its streets and homes were as safe as they could be. It was no mean feat, considering her remit covered most of Western Cornwall and the job took her from Helford to Land's

End, St Ives to Charlestown and back again on a daily basis.

Gabriel said nothing further, and perhaps his quiet patience was her undoing.

"It'll be public knowledge by now," she found herself saying, and that was true enough. Any one of the residents who were questioned that morning would have been eager to pick up the phone and tell three of their friends. "A body was discovered on Porthgwidden beach, first thing. We're treating the death as suspicious."

Unbidden, an image of his father's lifeless body flashed into his mind, and Gabriel shoved it away, locking it in the place where he kept all of his saddest memories.

"I'm sorry to hear it," he said, after a moment. "Anyone I know?"

Sophie could say no more without giving away sensitive details of an active investigation, aside from which they hadn't been able to make an identification yet.

"Once next of kin have been informed, we'll be speaking to everyone," she said.

He nodded. "You said 'suspicious'—does that mean there's a suggestion of foul play?"

Sophie thought of the little fish scored into the man's arm, and of the brutal blows to his skull. She thought of the kind of personality capable of inflicting that degree of harm, then she thought of a man with eyes the same shade as her own, who'd taught her to ride a bike.

A man who was, at this very moment, terminally ill and at large.

The kind of man who had nothing to lose.

"I—" She stood up, willing herself not to succumb to the nausea that churned in the pit of her stomach. "I'm sorry, I need to—to get back to work."

Gabriel was many things, but a fool was not one of them. He saw the clammy layer of sweat caking her skin, and heard the soft, panting breaths she was trying to conceal.

"Going back to the station?" he said, idly. "I'll walk with you."

"There's no need," she said, between gritted teeth. "I don't need a chaperone."

There was every need, he thought.

"What's the matter, Detective? Are you afraid people will talk?"

Her colour came back, very quickly.

"If they do, it'll be to say I'm bringing you in for *questioning,*" she snapped.

"Feel free to use the handcuffs when you do," he offered, having decided that anger was preferable to vulnerability, which was something neither of them was ready to show.

Sophie rounded on him, the action causing her leather satchel to swing around with such ferocity it narrowly missed hitting him.

"You're very sure of yourself, aren't you?"

Gabriel considered the question. "When it comes to some things, I am," he admitted, and took a step closer, crowding her just enough without it being *too* much. "I could say the same of you."

Sophie took her time reaching inside her bag to retrieve her own sunglasses, and settled them on her nose so he no longer had the advantage of being able to read her eyes.

"You don't know me at all," she said, firmly.

"But I will," he replied, and there was a brief, charged silence as the full impact of his words warmed her chilly veins.

"The only thing you're going to *know* is the business end of my *boot*," she snarled, and pointed towards the old pair of walking boots she wore. "Especially when it connects with your arse!"

"Police harassment and intimidation, now?"

She emitted a squeak—that was the only word to describe it—and was even more incensed.

"Well," he said, satisfied that his work was done. "If you feel like harassing me again later, I was thinking of having a bit of dinner over at The Sloop around seven-thirty, so that's where you'll find me."

He nodded towards an ancient pub overlooking the harbour, reputed to have been built in the early fourteenth century, which made it the oldest public house in town and one of the oldest in the country.

"I'll save you a seat, Detective."

With that, he turned and left, whistling a jazzy tune beneath his breath.

Sophie watched his retreating back, then swore volubly and marched herself back to the station with a face like thunder, the shame of her family lineage banished temporarily to the sea and sky.

CHAPTER 6

Judging from the speed at which Sophie covered the distance between the harbour and the police station, it was clear that a general sense of outrage was vastly more potent than rocket fuel. It carried her all the way to the entrance of the uninspiring structure that was her workplace, and she was still muttering to herself about the nerve of *that man,* with his innuendos about the improper usage of police handcuffs and God only knew what else, as she burst through its rusted, steel-framed doors.

She was met with the stench of stale alcohol, which called to mind the image of a jolly, red-faced man by the name of 'Terry', who'd often visited their house when she was little, before everything changed. He'd been friendly, never without a packet of chocolate buttons or a little toy of some description, but had often smelled like the inside of a brewery, as her father would say. Years later, when she'd taken the time to look up who 'Uncle Terry' really was, she learned he was the owner of a number of pubs and clubs in the North East of England, and had set up a lucrative drugs syndicate whereby the bouncers would double up as dealers or look out for them when they'd call in, spreading their poison through the hearts and minds of the young people out for a good time on a Friday or Saturday night. Terry and his syndicate had been directly responsible for the spread of crack cocaine through the streets of Newcastle, Sunderland and Middlesbrough throughout the nineties, creating a generation of addicts whose lives were utterly consumed.

No amount of chocolate buttons could make up for that.

Now, Sophie had learned to tolerate the smell of booze, but rarely touched the stuff because she preferred to remain in complete control at all times. She was not teetotal, but she had a reputation to uphold and, if life had taught her anything at all, it was that a good reputation was a rare commodity to acquire and an even rarer one to keep.

Nobody knew this better than the man who was, at that very moment, lying half-slumped on one of the visitors' chairs in the tiny foyer, under the watchful but weary eye of the desk sergeant.

"Hello, Eddie," she said to the source of the malodour. "Been up to mischief again?"

With some effort, he roused himself, and struggled into an upright position.

"Dunno what—what all the fuss is about," he said, and stifled a burp. "I was mindin' my own business, then some feller came along and—and—"

He trailed off, and gave an enormous, jaw-cracking yawn.

"He's been in overnight," the desk sergeant told her. "We're waiting for someone to come and pick him up."

"I was only—only tryin' to cheer everyone up, s'all. Where's the harm in that?"

Sophie sighed.

It was well known that Eddie liked a bit of a singsong after he'd passed the point of no return. For some, it was harmless fun, but, to a pub manager or the mother of a baby trying to sleep, it was a public nuisance.

"Have you spoken to your sponsor, lately?"

For a while, Eddie had been a regular member of Alcoholics Anonymous.

"Don't need to," he said, stubbornly. "I'm fine—abso—s'lutely fine. Don't know why you—you've got to get your knickers all in a twist—"

"Eddie."

There was a warning note to her voice, and he heard it.

"Sorry," he mumbled, and scrubbed his hands over his eyes. "I—I just—"

"I know," Sophie said, more gently this time. It was obvious, even without looking at the charge sheet, that he'd been brought in for causing a public disturbance, possibly being drunk and disorderly, but no amount of strong-arming, threats of prosecution or nights spent in a cell could rid Eddie of his terrible need for drink. That lived inside him, spreading like a sickness, but it could be managed and controlled with help and perseverance. Unfortunately, he'd alienated many of his family and friends, and public resources were already stretched to breaking point.

He needed a friend, as they all did, sometimes.

Sophie moved to sit on one of the chairs beside him, and thought briefly that she might have preferred the smell of the body they'd found that morning.

"You can turn things around," she said, as she'd done many times before. "It's never too late, Eddie. You can do this, if you really want to."

"Sarge?" PC Turner stuck his head around the door, and she nodded.

"Be there in a minute."

Twenty minutes later, she re-joined her team, having overseen Eddie's transfer into the safekeeping of his remaining family. She did not delude herself that it was the last time he'd be visiting the station, but if she had to go through the same routine all over again, she would.

There was always hope, and it was worth fighting for.

That was something else she'd learned from life.

———

As the sun began to dip low in the sky, Sophie leaned back in her chair, massaged the crick in her neck, and was forced to admit she'd done all she could to progress the open investigations littering her desktop. There were no further leads in the case of the missing painting and, more importantly, there'd been no eyewitness sightings or other pertinent evidence to help them to identify the man's body they'd found that morning. A check of her own list, as well as the national missing persons database, had elicited several possibilities—sad though it was, plenty of middle-aged men had been reported missing around the country, but she'd already eliminated a good number based on race, height, or other distinguishing features that couldn't possibly be a match for their 'John Doe'. It was unfortunate that so much of the man's skin had decomposed, because that made it harder to see the detail of what appeared to be a number of tattoos adorning his back and chest, but at least their existence helped to rule out missing persons without any ink. That still left a healthy number, none of whom appeared to hail from their corner of the world.

Once she'd spent some time trying to determine the victim's identity, she turned her attention to the perpetrator. A vision of an attractive man with hair the same shade as her own and dark, penetrating eyes sprang immediately into her mind, and she looked down at her hands, which boasted the same long, artistic fingers as her father's. But, where he'd used his to carve up people's skin and inflict hurt and terror into the hearts of those who'd crossed him or his gang, she'd done her best to wield them only for good.

"Mind if I head off now, Sarge?"

Turner stuck his head around the edge of his desktop monitor and, since his shift had ended over an hour ago, she nodded.

"You don't have to keep doing overtime, Alex," she said.

"I know." He stood up to stretch his back. "But you stay past your contractual hours often enough."

She didn't have a good answer for that, so she scowled at him instead.

"As I've told you a hundred times, 'Do as I say, not as I do'," she muttered. "Especially when it comes to having any kind of social life. I'm not the best example to follow."

He thought privately that she was one of the most dedicated public servants he'd ever had the privilege to work with, but to say as much would have embarrassed them both and, as it happened, he had a date with a handsome surf instructor by the name of Patrick, whom he'd met while doing some of the door-to-doors that very morning.

Sometimes the uniform helped.

"You should get out more," he did say. "There's a live band playing at The Sloop, tonight."

"Will everyone stop trying to get me to go to The Sloop!" she burst out, with more vehemence than was necessary.

It was enough to pique her constable's interest. "Somebody's already asked you along, then?"

"That's none of your damned business, Turner, and I'll thank you to bugger off."

He grinned. "Enjoy yourself," he said. "It's Friday night, after all."

Was it?

She was not like her constable, who was able to compartmentalise his work while his mind focused on happier things.

Sophie thought again of the fish, and her stomach performed a slow somersault.

"Have a good evening, and I'll see you tomorrow—it may be the weekend, but crime never sleeps, and neither do we."

He laughed, but cast one final, concerned glance in her direction. "You—"

"Goodnight, Turner."

"Yes, ma'am."

CHAPTER 7

The Sloop was nothing short of an institution.

With low ceilings, dark beams and exposed stonework, it brimmed with character and indeed *characters*, ranging from well-heeled businessmen to working fishermen, local artists and musicians, and everything in between. History lived and breathed within its gnarly walls and, as Gabriel dipped inside its cosy, bustling interior, he had a funny notion of having stepped back in time; it might have been two hundred years earlier and the vibrant sense of community would have been the same as that very day. The fashions might have changed, but the thrum of conversation and laughter was timeless.

The public space was loosely divided into two main bar areas at the front and back, separated by an archway, and a third area which was accessed through a wooden swing door and was usually reserved for dining. The bar occupied a central apex, its polished wooden counter forming a circle around which the three areas were serviced equally by roaming staff who could keep a weather eye on their patrons from every angle.

As he entered the main bar, Gabriel experienced a number of different emotions.

The first was a sense of familiarity; the little pub was, after all, only a few hundred metres along the wharf from his family home and had been a part of his childhood from his earliest memory.

The second was anger; a white-hot, impotent rage. It was here that his father had chosen to drink himself into an early grave, until his illness had become obvious, and the staff had discharged an admirable duty of care, refusing to serve him any longer. Left to his own devices, John Rowe

73

had turned the living room of their home into his own private drinking hole, with pictures of his beloved wife still sitting on the mantelpiece. Slowly, he drowned himself, until his effort became a reality one fateful night and ended the cycle of alcoholism that would have taken him somewhere, somehow, in the end.

Or so he'd always believed.

Gabriel's final thought, after the tidal wave had abated, was disappointment. Of all the faces that turned to stare at him with open curiosity, the one he'd been hoping to see was the only one missing from their number.

Sophie had not come.

"Gabriel Rowe, as I live and breathe!"

He turned to find a man standing before him balancing a tray of glasses. He was around sixty, dressed in smart clothes that were beginning to crease along with his face, which bore the reddish flush of one who was already onto his fourth pint.

"Mr Trenthorn," he said, keeping his voice light. "It's been a long time."

Arthur Trenthorn owned several restaurants and cafés in the local area, including a down-to-earth fish and chip shop, where people stopped in to pick up some battered fish and fried chips they could eat beside the harbour—if the gulls didn't get their beaks in there first. There was also an upmarket French bistro, a Michelin-starred restaurant specialising in local produce and various other ventures, probably many more that Gabriel didn't know about. Despite easy access to an abundance of dining options, Trenthorn remained slim, his diet being subject to the careful management of his wife—with the exception of the Friday night 'Pie and Pint' he routinely enjoyed with a group of friends he'd known since boyhood. Above all this, Arthur Trenthorn had once been his father's best friend.

Now, he beamed at Gabriel, visibly moved by the sight of the boy he'd known towering above him now, a grown man.

"I wondered if we'd be seeing you," he said, and his eyes searched Gabriel's face, noticing the line of jaw that was so similar to his friend's, the shade of his eyes, and even the shape of his hands. "I was going to stop by, but—"

He trailed off, uncertain as to the kind of response he'd receive. A lot of water had passed beneath that particular bridge, but some memories didn't fade as easily as they should.

"I understand," Gabriel said, and he did.

He understood that Arthur Trenthorn had seen his friend's little boy in the very depths of despair, and had come to his own conclusions about the veracity of what he had to say about his father's death—namely, that he hadn't been so drunk as to stumble off the edge of a pier. It was easy to label a ten-year-old as 'confused', especially one who'd idolised his father and would have done and said almost anything to protect him, even in death.

"I always wanted to tell you, I'm sorry about what happened—"

Gabriel interrupted him. "It's over and done with," he said, and told his second lie of the day. "I was just a kid; I didn't know what I was saying."

Arthur nodded, heaved a long sigh, then indicated a table on the far side of the room. "Why not sit and join us for a pint? Tell us what you've been doing, all these years."

It might have been interesting to reacquaint himself with the men who circled one of the scarred wooden tables but, just then, the door to the main bar opened and a far better offer presented itself.

"Thanks, but I have other plans," he murmured.

With that, he turned away and left Arthur Trenthorn to watch his progress across the room, wondering where all the years had gone and why, despite their passage, it might have been only yesterday that John Rowe had stood in the place his son now occupied.

———

Sophie needn't have worried she'd have any trouble picking Gabriel Rowe out of the Friday-night crowd. His height was above average, for one thing, but, as he made his way towards her, she acknowledged there was more to the man than mere physicality. There was a focused, watchful air about him that gave the impression of a man who knew exactly what he wanted and how to get it.

At that moment, the object of his focus was *her*.

A lesser woman might have felt a degree of nerves in the face of that kind of overt attention, but since she most definitely didn't fall into that category, Sophie attributed the churning feeling in her stomach to hunger pangs and nothing more.

Not *that* kind of hunger…

Oh, all right, she amended.

It *had* been a while since she'd eaten.

"Hungry?"

For one short, horrified moment, Sophie thought she'd spoken aloud. "What?"

Gabriel smiled. "I asked whether you were feeling hungry," he said. "I assume by your presence here that you've decided to take up my offer of a bite to eat—while you grill me about my nefarious past, of course."

The last part was said in a light-hearted tone that implied he had nothing of the kind but, since she was by nature a suspicious being and he looked downright suspicious at the best of times, Sophie decided to reserve judgment.

"I often drop in," she said. "Besides, there's no harm in being neighbourly, is there?"

"None at all," he agreed, and placed a casual hand in the crook of her arm, leading her towards the dining area where he'd booked a table for their 'neighbourly' dinner.

Sophie felt the eyes of the town watching them and, as much as she found the warm weight of his hand oddly comforting through the layer of her jacket, she would have shrugged it away, had he not chosen that moment to remove it and hold open the door to the dining room instead.

"Everything all right?"

He was looking at her with a quizzical expression, no doubt wondering why she'd come to a ridiculous standstill.

"Yes," she muttered. "Sorry, it's been a long day."

And it was rare for a man to hold a door open for her, she might have added. *Or take her arm, and ask if she was all right.*

Sophie would never have described herself as a 'romantic'. She'd seen enough of the darker side of life to be warned against it. Quite apart from her daily brushes with the criminal world, being a living witness to her mother's misplaced love for a man who'd turned out to be unworthy in the extreme had served as a stark warning.

Don't make the same mistakes I did, Sophie, she'd often say. *No man can be trusted.*

As for the male friendships she'd managed to develop, they tended to be with unattainable men who presented no threat to her equilibrium. Take Luke, or Nick…they were both wonderful men, very much in love with their chosen partners. As for Alex, her workmate and general dogsbody, she was the wrong gender, and, in any case, she treated him much in the same way she might have done a younger brother.

In short, Sophie had built up a safe and secure circle of friends and colleagues, and was very happy with the status quo. If she felt lonely from time to time, there'd been very occasional liaisons that provided a temporary salve and lasted no more than a few months. No hard feelings when it ended, and no heartache either.

Now, she found herself standing on the threshold of a doorway to the unknown. Beyond it, there was more than just a dining room decorated with candles and carnations—that much was obvious.

"Shall we?"

Sophie looked up into his face, and felt the same mix of fear and excitement she'd experienced from their first meeting.

"I think I'll have the scampi," she said, and stepped through the door.

CHAPTER 8

"Tell me about yourself, Detective."

Sophie stared at him over the rim of her wine glass and took another sip of what was, she had to admit, a very nice Chablis.

Just one glass, she warned herself.

"I'm usually the one to ask the questions," she said, trotting out a line she'd often employed to deflect attention away from herself. "Besides, I'm far more interested in finding out about other people. For instance, what is it you do for a living, Gabriel?"

"I'm a writer," he said, happy to take her lead. "I tell stories for a living."

In the soft candlelight of a former smugglers' den, he fit the stereotypical mould of a writer of dark thrillers, she thought, or perhaps crime fiction—she'd heard they were a suspicious bunch.

"Would I have read any of them?"

"That depends," he said, with a smile. "Do you have any children between the ages of eight and twelve?"

Children? She almost choked.

Unexpectedly, the image of a baby with dark hair and laughing blue eyes popped into her mind, and she set her glass down on the table with a clatter.

"*No*," she said, firmly. "I don't have any kids. What does that have to do with anything?"

"I write adventure novels for children," he said, and didn't bother to mention that they'd sold in their millions. "About secrets, smugglers, pirates and treasure maps...everything I used to imagine when I was a kid."

Sophie made an urgent reassessment of the man seated in front of her. "You...write books for kids?"

He laughed at the expression on her face, which was one of pure bafflement. "Yes, what did you think I was going to say?"

Sophie lifted a shoulder, and picked up her wine glass again—which a passing server had helpfully refilled. "Oh, I don't know. Used car salesman, maybe?

Gabriel smiled slowly, and thanked the young woman who stopped by to clear their plates. When they were alone again, he leaned forward with a gleam in his eye. "Do I look like the kind of man who could sell you a ride, Sophie?"

Her heart gave one solid thud against the wall of her chest, and she took several deep breaths before responding. "You look as though you could sell anything to anybody," she admitted quietly. "That's a dangerous skill to possess."

She thought of another man with boundless charm, who'd held her on his shoulders and taken her to ballet classes on Saturdays. Everyone always had a friendly wave for Mick Gallagher, at least until his house of cards had come tumbling down.

Fear wasn't the same as respect, when all was said and done.

Her next thought was of the dead man they'd found on the beach that morning, and her eyes darted around the dining room, searching for a face she recognised...the face of a killer.

Gabriel's words had been playful, but he sensed they'd touched a nerve, for the laughter had gone from her eyes and he was sorry for it. Now, she seemed on edge, as though she expected someone to jump at her from the shadows. Watching the play of emotions across her face, he wondered what she was thinking.

"You've nothing to worry about," he said, and stole a hand across the table to brush her fingers. "I might write stories about the occasional bad guy, but I don't happen to be one myself."

When his skin touched hers, her body came alive, and made a mockery of his statement.

There was *everything* to worry about.

"Where do you get your ideas?" she asked, in a rush to change the subject.

Gabriel leaned back again, breaking the contact. "Here, there, everywhere," he said, with a shrug. "I remember a lot of the bedtime stories my father used to tell me. He was a wonderful storyteller."

His voice had softened again, she thought, and was warm with remembered affection.

"He sounds like a wonderful man," Sophie said, and felt a small pang of jealousy.

What would it feel like, to be proud of her father?

That was something she'd never know.

"Nobody is perfect," Gabriel surprised her by saying. "I have many happy memories of him but, in his last couple of years, there are plenty of others I'd rather forget."

Now, she leaned forward. "I'm sorry," she mumbled. "It must have been awful for you—"

"Life is full of darkness and light, don't you think?" he said, rubbing his fingers idly across hers. "It's character building, or so people say."

"Is it?" she wondered aloud.

She supposed that, without her own unique experience, she wouldn't have been driven to enter the police force. She also wouldn't be so lonely and shut off from the world.

She took another sip of wine.

"Why are you really here, Gabriel?"

Something flickered behind his eyes, before they became shuttered again. "I'm here to enjoy the company of a beautiful woman," he said simply.

She told herself not to be flattered by that, or distracted from her line of questioning.

"I don't mean *here*," she said, gesturing around the dining room. "I mean, *here* in St Ives. Why did you choose to come back now?"

He made a show of reaching for his own glass, and took a healthy slug, to give himself time to think. "I was invited to do a signing at the St Ives Bookseller," he said, referring to a quaint little bookshop a few streets over. "I have a new book out, so it seemed like a good time to accept."

It all seemed very plausible, she thought. Why, then, didn't she believe him?

"Has there been any update on the missing painting?" he asked, in a smooth change of direction. "I liked the look of that one."

"Why?"

He cocked his head, and gave a lazy smile that didn't quite reach his eyes. "It features Wharf House in the composition," he said. "I liked the way the artist captured the bay, with moonlight falling over the harbour and the house."

It wasn't *untrue*, and yet, it wasn't wholly *true*, either.

"Perhaps you could commission a copy from the artist directly," she suggested. "I plan to speak with Mr Mostend tomorrow, so I can pass on your details if you'd like."

Gabriel thought about whether to mention that he'd already tried to pay Dean Mostend a visit, without success.

"Please do," was all he said. "You have a lot on your plate at the moment," he observed.

She knew he wasn't talking about the scampi, which hadn't touched the sides.

"No more than usual," she said.

He thought of how pale she'd looked earlier, and wondered if that was true.

"Some days are harder than others, and that's true of any profession," he said, thinking of times when the words just wouldn't flow onto a page. "It must be particularly true of yours."

He was speaking of the body they'd found, and of the carousel of thefts, assaults and drug-related crimes she dealt with in any given week, but that wasn't what weighed her down each day.

It was the *past*, and its constant impact on the present.

Twenty-five years was a long time to keep a secret; such a *very* long time to bear the burden of guilt and shame of who she really was, and live amongst people as an impostor. Sophie longed to find someone with whom she could be herself without fear of judgment or reprisals. There was her mother, but whenever the topic of their shared past arose, it tended to open Pandora's box and there followed hours and days of tears and remembered trauma. The roles were reversed, and Sophie was invariably the one to console her mother—not the other way around. She'd learned it was easier to shoulder her own feelings and allow her mother to continue life in the happy bubble she created for herself.

She'd been through enough, and deserved her own happy ending.

She realised Gabriel was waiting for some kind of response, and it was on the tip of her tongue to dish out some platitude or another.

"It's character building," she said, with a crooked smile. "There's a lot of darkness in my life, Gabriel. You should know that."

He was silent for a moment, but when he spoke, his words resonated.

"Mine too," he said. "That only means that, when we find a bit of light, we have to hold on to it. Don't you think?"

Sophie ignored the fuzziness in her brow, the slight blurring at the edge of her vision, and enjoyed the happy, mellow feeling of being relaxed in his company. It had been a long time and, as Turner had suggested, it was Friday night, and she should let her hair down a bit.

Others might be dead, but she wasn't—not yet, at least.

CHAPTER 9

The next morning

Sophie awoke to the smell of freshly brewed coffee.

She basked in its sweet aroma for all of ten seconds before sitting bolt upright, fully alert and questioning how Mr Bigglesworth, her cat, could possibly have developed the dexterity to brew coffee.

A swift recce of her surroundings confirmed her worst suspicion.

She was not at home.

She lay back in the crumpled white sheets—soft, silky, high-thread-count sheets—of an enormous, super-king bed. The room was dimly lit, the light of the morning leaking around the edges of several picture windows shielded by tasteful Roman blinds, but she could see white walls and rustic oak furniture, pretty pictures on the walls and, most damningly, no sign of her clothes.

With a sharp intake of breath, she looked down, and found she was wearing an over-sized white t-shirt displaying a faded *Baywatch* motif and a slogan which read, "DON'T HASSLE THE HOFF!"

A further inspection confirmed she was, at least, still in possession of her underwear.

A dull but persistent throb hammered at her temples and the base of her skull and, even as she formulated the tirade of angry words she would unleash upon Gabriel Rowe, she snatched up the box of aspirin and glass of water he'd left on the bedside table for her, muttering darkly as she swallowed a couple of pills to ease the grip of a brutal hangover.

Fuelled by pride and indignation, she swung her legs off the bed, closed her eyes as the action brought with it a fresh wave of aches and pains, and then rose to her feet.

The room swayed as if she stood on a boat's deck, then righted itself.

Marching into the adjoining bathroom, she was even more outraged to find he'd left a fresh toothbrush out for her, and fluffy white towels folded neatly on a wicker chair.

"The nerve," she muttered, before making full use of them.

Dressed in the cosy white dressing gown he'd also left for her, and having washed away any trace of the previous evening, Sophie prepared to face her attacker—right before she slapped a pair of handcuffs on his arrogant wrists and marched him through the streets of St Ives. She didn't know what happened between them the previous evening, her memory having fallen off sometime after dinner, but she was certain she hadn't legally consented to it.

Whatever it was.

Downstairs, Gabriel glanced at the ceiling above his head, which thudded in time to a series of angry footsteps, grinned to himself, and took another sip of the coffee he'd just made.

It was going to be an interesting morning.

A couple of minutes later, she appeared in the kitchen doorway, swathed in his dressing gown which was slightly too large. Her hair was freshly washed and hung damply around her head, and her face was free of make-up which, despite her exploits the night before, still managed to look as fresh as a daisy.

Or, at least, as fresh as a daisy that'd had a bit too much to drink and was now suffering the after-effects.

"Morning," he said, cheerfully. "Fancy a coffee?"

Sophie's eyes narrowed, first on him and his insufferably handsome face, then on the mug he held out to her.

"What's in it, this time?" she threw out. "You must think I've lost my mind, if you think I'd accept another drink from you."

For Gabriel, surprise gave way to an anger that was cold and hard. "I beg your pardon?"

She folded her arms, and studiously ignored the wounded look on his face which—she had to admit—looked completely genuine.

Pathological liars were always believable.

"You heard me, Mr Rowe. Now, I'd like my clothes back, before we go for a chat—down at the station."

Just like that, anger circled back around to humour, and his body relaxed against the kitchen counter. "I *see*," he said, drawing the words out. "I take it you don't remember the latter part of our evening, so you've assumed the worst?"

"You know *fine well* that I don't—and what else am I to assume?"

He wondered how to break things to her gently, and wondered whether she deserved it, since she'd demonstrated such a shabby opinion of him.

Tempting though it was to play up to her imaginary demons, he decided the truth was the safest route.

"I'd stop jumping to conclusions and hurling accusations, if I were you," he said mildly. "I was given to understand people were presumed innocent in this country."

"You're as guilty as sin," she muttered. "Now, give me my clothes back."

The conversation wasn't finished, not by a long shot, but he turned and moved into an adjoining utility room, where he'd recently finished washing and drying the clothes she'd vomited on the night before.

"Here you go," he said, and she snatched them from his open hand.

Sophie smelled fresh detergent, something pleasantly unflowery, and jumped to the next conclusion.

"Destroying evidence now, as well?"

Gabriel took another slug of coffee and told himself to remain calm, even if she was maligning his character in the very worst way.

"If, by 'evidence', you're referring to the remains of your scampi and chips, then yes," he bit out. "I assumed you'd rather not wear vomit-stained clothing on your way home."

The mention of sickness elicited a flash memory of them leaving the pub the previous evening, and having found the night air a shock to her system...

Then...

Then...

"Oh, God," she whispered. "I was sick in one of the bins outside The Sloop."

Gabriel pulled a face, and nodded.

"In the main, you were very neat about it, but your jeans didn't quite escape the onslaught."

It all came back to her then, like the reel of a bad movie.

First, Gabriel suggesting she drink some water or have a coffee before they leave, both of which she refused. Then, Gabriel suggesting it was time she went home, and asking whether he could call a taxi for her or escort her back himself.

Choosing neither option, she'd dragged them both to the tiny dance floor where the band had begun to play some old seventies classics. She had a fleeting image of his arms around her—holding her upright, as much as anything else—before guiding her gently from the pub.

"I did ask whether you'd like to be taken home," he said, breaking the silence. "You wouldn't give me your home address, so I couldn't take you there. I didn't think you would want anybody to see you while you were—*ah*—not quite yourself, so I thought it best to bring you back here and let you sleep it off."

Sophie remembered now, with painful clarity.

"You looked after me," she whispered. "You made sure nobody saw me...in that state."

He nodded. "I'm sorry, I had to help you undress, because your clothes needed to be washed. I'm also sorry that the Baywatch t-shirt was the first thing to hand."

Her lips twitched, a brief respite from the harrowing shame of it all.

"I don't know what to say."

"Don't say anything, and have a coffee instead," he suggested, topping off a fresh mug which he handed to her. "What about something stodgy— bacon sarnie?"

The thought of food made her shudder inside the dressing gown, and his ongoing kindness shamed her all the more.

"I don't know if I'll ever be able to eat again."

She swallowed the first, fortifying gulp of coffee, and asked the question she needed to ask for her own peace of mind.

"I'm sorry to have to ask this, but…"

"No, Sophie, we didn't," he interrupted her. "Call me old fashioned, but when I take a woman to bed, I prefer her to be *compos mentis*."

Ever the gentleman, he said nothing of the rest.

"Thank you," she said simply, and gulped the rest of her coffee, scalding her throat in the process. "For everything," she added.

"My pleasure," he replied. "You're a happy drunk, if it makes you feel any better."

She groaned, and almost held her head in her hands. "I hardly ever drink," she said. "I don't know what came over me. Such a stupid, dangerous thing to do."

"It isn't a crime to have a drink or two on a Friday night, Sophie," he told her. "As for getting a bit merry, that doesn't make you stupid, it makes you human. And as for 'dangerous'—"

His voice faltered, as a picture of his father caught his peripheral vision.

"There was no danger," he finished quietly. "I was with you, and I'd never let you fall."

She looked up and into his face, which was averted as he looked out of the window, his mind far away from the little kitchen where they stood.

And yet, she could guess what he was thinking, this man she hardly knew.

He was thinking that, if he'd been with his father that fateful night, he would never have let him fall.

"You aren't responsible," she said quietly.

He turned back, an easy smile back on his face once more. "For you? I know you can look after yourself, Detective—"

"I don't mean for me."

Gabriel stared at her, into eyes that were full of understanding, and then set his cup down on the countertop. "Would you say you were fully sober now, Sophie?"

She saw the change in him, felt the shift in the room, and her heart rate quickened. "Yes," she said.

He took a step closer, and then another, until they stood toe to toe.

"In that case, do you have any objection to my kissing you?"

She shook her head, and his hands moved to hold her arms lightly, while his head lowered.

Just before their lips touched, he pulled back.

"Wait—did you remember to brush your teeth?"

Outraged again, she prepared to say something suitably cutting, but the words never made it past his lips, which captured hers with a low rumble of laughter.

CHAPTER 10

Jacqui Keane had come a long way since she was Kim Gallagher.

Some days, she could almost convince herself that woman never existed at all. Twenty-five years had cemented a new life in Cornwall, one she was very grateful to have and would do anything to keep. She could still remember the first day they'd arrived in St Ives, all those years ago. The poky, one-bedroom flat with rising damp and peeling paint provided by the Witness Protection Service; the lashing rain—so far removed from what they'd been led to believe would await them at the end of a ten-hour drive.

Where's the sunshine? Sophie had asked.

And then, as if by magic, it had appeared.

Rather than spend time cleaning or unpacking their meagre belongings, she'd snatched up her little daughter and run down to the beach to make footprints in the sand.

She wondered if Sophie would remember that.

There had been so much upheaval, so much hurt and confusion for a child of four, and she'd struggled, too; a young woman without home or family, having just learned the very worst news about the man with whom she'd laughed and loved and shared her bed. He'd fathered her child, the most precious thing in her world, and for that simple reason she could not bring herself to hate him—at least, not as much as she might have done, without Sophie.

It was hard, sometimes, to look at her daughter and see so much of Mick reflected in the shade of her eyes, or in an expression she might pull... Lord, even in the way Sophie smiled—which was rare.

Too rare, for a mother's comfort.

If she had one wish, it would be for her child to be happy. Wasn't that what all decent parents wanted for their children? Oh, she knew that Sophie would say she was perfectly happy with life. She'd launch into a long, practised spiel about how she didn't need a partner to be happy, and wasn't it awful that women were under so much pressure to find a man, as if they couldn't be enough on their own. If she was really on a roll, she'd talk about social conditioning and toxic, anti-feminist traits pervading modern society.

Jacqui sighed, and reached for another cardboard box to unpack. This time, it was a selection of fragrant candles, which she arranged in a pretty formation on one of the glass shelves fitted around Scents of Cornwall, the shop she owned in the centre of town.

There was no question a woman could survive on her own—hadn't she proven that, herself?—but there was also nothing wrong in hoping to find somebody to love, and share the ups and downs of life. It was something she'd hoped for, as a younger woman, but with age had come acceptance. Oh, there had been plenty of offers over the years, some of which she'd seriously considered. But, when a heart had been burned as badly as hers, nothing and nobody could heal the wound. It festered, a constant ache that never went away, although the pain that had once been raw had dimmed with the passage of time. Busy-work, first as a cleaner, then as the owner of her own cleaning company with a full staff of employees, and finally as the owner of a boutique shop selling artisan, organic cleaning products, toiletries and candles had provided ample distraction over the years. Industry had enabled her to buy a little cottage, a fixer-upper, which she and Sophie had lived in until her daughter left for university at eighteen. She remembered that had been a hard day; their bond had been so tight, so unbreakable, and her fear still so great, it had taken every ounce of self-control not to beg her daughter to stay.

Stay with me, where I can watch over you.

Stay here, where you're safe, in the cocoon I've built for us.

Stay in St Ives, where nobody can find you and hurt you.

Words she'd never said, because Sophie might have listened and stayed to make her mother happy. She'd never have become the strong, confident butterfly she was today; a pillar of the community, fearless and unafraid to walk into the shadowy corners of the world.

Unlike Kim, who was still so terribly afraid, and always would be.

But Jacqui? Jacqui could be vivacious, running the shop, chatting with customers, dealing with staff and suppliers, volunteering as a school governor and a trustee of various local charities. So long as Kim remembered to be Jacqui, everything would be all right.

She stood there for long minutes, staring sightlessly at the shelf with its pretty display, and then gave in to the compulsion she fought against each day.

She checked the lock on the front door, just to be sure.

Once.

Twice.

A few more times.

Thankfully, the shop wasn't open yet, because she needed more time to banish Kim to the recesses of her mind, where she belonged.

While her mother wrestled with two competing versions of herself, Sophie put the finishing touches to a murder board she'd set up at one end of the single conference room at the police station. Indeed, 'conference room' was a generous title for what was a glorified cupboard. The whole building was a temporary measure—a stopgap, so she'd been told—while a larger and better-equipped modern building was erected. However, following a brief conversation with a member of the construction team on site, who'd told her the new facility would be ready 'dreckly', she wasn't holding her breath that its doors would be opening any time soon. While construction continued, she instructed her staff to settle in for the long haul.

"Morning, Sarge."

She turned to greet PC Turner, and with admirable *schadenfreude*, was delighted to find there was a person alive who looked and probably felt even worse than she did.

"Morning, Alex. How's the head?"

"Hammering like a demented woodpecker," he replied, without pause. "How's yours?"

"I should write you up for insubordination for even suggesting I might be suffering from the worst hangover known to all of mankind past and present," she said. "As it is, I'll commend you for having such acute observational skills."

Turner chuckled, and drew back a chair. Considering it was still just the two of them, he decided to chance a bit of gentle banter.

"I saw you at the pub last night," he said, idly.

Her hand stilled on the whiteboard, before continuing to scribble with a furious squeak of pen on plastic.

"Come on, then," she said. "Get it off your chest."

He grinned at her stiffened back. "Well, there were a couple of things that were noteworthy," he said, and began ticking them off his fingers. "In the first place, your date was hot. *Seriously* hot."

"Duly noted," she said, and experienced a pleasant little shiver at the memory of his lips on hers less than an hour before. "And, again, excellent observational skills."

"Thank you, ma'am," he said gravely. "And, at this point, I'd like to go on record and say that, if his preference for strong brunettes should ever extend beyond heterosexual norms, I'm available."

"I'll pass on the message," she said.

"Secondly, you've been hiding your dancing feet under a bushel, if last night's rendition of *Cotton Eye Joe* is anything to go by."

Sophie thanked her lucky stars the band hadn't chosen to play the Macarena.

Small mercies.

"Anytime you want some pointers on your cha-cha, just say the word."

Turner grinned again. "Finally, I'd say the aforementioned Hot Date is also a gentleman," he remarked, and left the rest unsaid.

"Tell me the truth, Alex. How bad was I, last night?" Sophie set aside her marker pen and turned to face him.

"To be honest, Sarge, you looked *happy*, which was nice to see."

She gave him a lopsided smile, and extra points for loyalty and discretion.

"You know what would make me happy—aside from country dancing, of course? Catching a killer, identifying a body, and finding a missing painting, all before lunchtime. Since that's unlikely to happen, I'll settle for another couple of aspirin and a strong black coffee."

Turner made a sound to convey his agreement. "You get the tablets, I'll get the coffee. Teamwork makes the dream work."

"Okay. Just one thing?"

"Hm?"

"Come out with a cheesy phrase like that within my earshot again, and I'm sending your arse straight back to highway patrol."

"Right you are."

CHAPTER 11

The harbour master watched a tall man in his mid-thirties stroll along the pier until he came to a particular point in the weathered stone near the very end, whereupon he stopped and moved perilously close to the edge—so close, the toes of his shoes rested on nothing but air.

"Hey! Step back—it's slippery over there!"

Gabriel looked up sharply at the sound of his voice and dutifully stepped back from the edge, before turning to face the newcomer, who was not new to him at all.

"Hello, Tom."

Tom Cutter came to a surprised halt, his eyes widening as though he'd seen a ghost.

"It can't be young Gabe Rowe—can it?"

Gabe was a shortened version of his name which had often been used during his childhood, and Gabriel hadn't answered to it for a very long time. It was distant echo from the past, like the pier beneath his feet and the older man standing slack-jawed in front of him.

"One and the same," he said. "It's been a long time."

"I heard you'd come back," Tom said, and took a step closer, inspecting Gabriel's face as if to check it was real and not some apparition his mind had conjured up.

By God, he was the spitting double of John.

Gabriel spread his arm in a wide arc to encompass the vista of turquoise blue sea and azure skies that surrounded them. "Things don't change much around here," he said. "The colours are unlike anything else in the world."

"Pretty enough," was all Tom would say. The sea was his master; he watched its undulations and changing moods as closely as he would a newborn baby.

"You wouldn't think we'd had a storm just the other night," Gabriel continued. "The sea's as calm as bathwater this morning."

Tom thought of the storm damage, and grunted. "Heard a man washed up, over on Porthgwidden," he said, and stuck his hands in his pockets. "Every blessed year, I tell them to show the sea some respect. They never listen."

Gabriel made a murmuring sound of agreement. "You don't think they were local, then?"

Tom shrugged his massive, workman's shoulders. "Couldn't say, but it's more'n likely to be someone from up-country."

Gabriel smiled, and wondered whether he would fall into that category of outsider, nowadays.

"Haven't seen you back here for a long while," Tom said, reading his mind. "Come to sell up, I expect?"

"Perhaps," Gabriel said, and thought of the other house he owned in Charlestown, a lovely old merchant's townhouse built during the Georgian period, which he'd hardly lived in. His had been a nomadic existence for the past decade, which had mostly been spent travelling the world meeting his young fans, all of whom were desperate for the next instalment of his series of Cornish adventures.

"I've come to lay some ghosts to rest, Tom. It's been twenty-seven years since my father passed away, but his death still feels unresolved. I want to lay him to rest in my own way."

Tom wasn't sure what to make of that, but turned to face the man who'd once been a boy nipping at his heels, learning about life on the water. "Never did believe that he fell, did you?"

Gabriel's eyes were shielded by sunglasses, and consequently his expression was unreadable.

However, when he spoke, his tone was unequivocal. "No," he said flatly. "I didn't."

Tom looked away, out across the water, and the two men stood in comfortable silence for a few minutes, each lost in their own memories of the past.

"When it happened, I believed what many believed," the harbour master said, choosing his words with care. "You're a man now, so I won't whitewash things. You know your old dad liked a drink, God rest him."

Gabriel nodded, for it was only the truth.

"When they found him, an accident seemed the most obvious explanation," Tom continued. "There was no foul play, nothing suspicious, according to the police and—"

He paused, wondering how far to go.

"Say it," Gabriel urged him. "You don't have to mollycoddle me."

Tom gave a short nod. "I saw him, washed up on the rocks, Gabe. It was bad, but nothing you wouldn't have expected from a night spent in the water, and that's the truth."

Gabriel thought of the records he'd managed to obtain, the coroner's report at the time, and knew that a verdict of 'death by misadventure' had been recorded, or, more colloquially, they thought John Rowe had died accidentally by his own actions. He might have believed it, could almost have convinced himself it was the case, were it not for the voices.

Hearing voices again, Gabe?

People had told him he must have been dreaming or imagining things, that night. He couldn't possibly have heard his father, alive and well, arguing with another man down on the beach at the foot of their house. It was fabrication, something his grieving heart had dreamt up to comfort him and try to provide a more palatable reason for his father's death. That's what everyone had said.

Arthur Trenthorn.
Tom Cutter.

Harry Pearce.

Derek Tailor.

They were his father's closest friends, the most likely to have been down on the beach with him on the night he died.

Yet none of them had admitted having any such meeting in their witness statements to the police. According to Arthur, Tom, Harry and Derek, they were each at home with their families without any knowledge of what young Gabe Rowe was talking about—but, of course, they were all very sorry when they heard what had happened to John.

I heard someone, Mr Pearce! I heard him talking to someone, and they were angry with him! Maybe they pushed him in the water...

Now, then, Gabe, that's a very big accusation to make—

I'm telling the truth!

But, as Gabriel had come to learn, truth was an awfully rare commodity.

"Do you still think I imagined overhearing an argument?" he asked Tom Cutter, as he would ask all of them, again and again, until he found the weakest link.

Tom turned, and put a hand on his shoulder.

"I think you should let your father rest in peace, son," he said quietly. "It's time you moved on from this—for your own sake."

Gabriel nodded, and shortly afterwards bade farewell to another of his father's old friends, watching him amble back along the pier, head bent against the wind that rushed up over the harbour wall.

He looked back down at the jagged rocks on the seaward side of the pier, and thought of a man who'd loved chess and playing games of Trivial Pursuit, paddle-boarding and watching the sun set over the water. Then, he remembered his father's body, nothing but an empty shell washed up on the rocks, ripe for others to pick over. As a child, he'd been powerless to prevent it, but not now.

Not now, nor ever again.

CHAPTER 12

A few streets from where Gabriel contemplated his next steps, DS Keane contemplated hers.

The conference cupboard was, by then, full to brimming with the entirety of police staff assigned to the murder investigation, which consisted of herself and PC Turner, who would act as Reader-Receiver, an intelligence analyst by the name of Liz, who worked from home three days per week, access to forensics and digital forensics support staff out of Bodmin HQ, as well as the approval to commandeer a couple of local bobbies based out of other nearby offices if necessary.

In short, the officers in attendance at the briefing were the same two that had been there at the beginning of the day, both of whom had imbibed a skinful of caffeine to offset their combined alcohol consumption the night before, and whose innate professionalism prevented either of them from allowing it to affect their concentration.

To help matters, the single desk fan had been set to 'maximum'.

At the head of the room, Sophie had set up a Murder Board, upon which she'd written a crude timeline of events alongside the facts as they knew them, and had tacked up a printed photograph of the victim's forearm beside it, detailing the carved image of a fish. Usually, it would be a picture of his face, but his was unrecognisable.

"Let's recap what we know so far," she began by saying. "The body of a man aged approximately forty-five to sixty-five was discovered on Porthgwidden beach yesterday morning, by a local woman, Dawn Musgrove, who was out walking her dog—"

Just then, the outer door swung open, and Detective Chief Superintendent Harry Pearce entered the room. He was a tall, wiry man with a thatch of salt-and-pepper grey hair cut in a short, military style. Straight-backed and with a year-round tan, he was sixty-one but could easily have passed for ten years younger.

"Sorry for the intrusion DS Keane, PC Turner," he said, peremptorily. "I thought I would sit in on your briefing. I'll have half the neighbourhood banging my door down for answers, this evening, and I want to know what I shouldn't be telling them."

Sophie smiled politely, and indicated one of two remaining chairs.

"Of course, sir. We were only just getting started."

He nodded, pinched his slacks at the knees to hike them up an inch, and then sat down. Her eyes were drawn by the action, and she was reminded of her maternal grandfather who often did the same thing to protect the material of his trousers from wearing thin at the knees. When they'd entered the Witness Protection Scheme, she and her mother agreed to cut ties with her grandparents, and it had been one of the most difficult rules to keep. It had also been one of the first rules she'd consciously *broken* when, aged eighteen, she'd defied her mother and gone in search of them.

Their reunion had been tearful, but immediate.

They were due to visit Cornwall at the end of the summer. At their advancing age, she wasn't sure how many more visits would be possible, and Sophie planned to try once again to convince them to stay in Cornwall for good, where she and her mother could look after them both and be a family once more.

But that was a matter for another day.

"I was just saying that the victim has not yet been identified," she told her DCS. "DNA and dental enquiries have been made, and are being processed as we speak. Turnaround time is currently seventy-two hours, but I'm told they might be able to get something back to us by close of business tomorrow, if we're lucky."

If there was an implied plea for extra resources to be able to pay for an express forensic service, DCS Pearce ignored it. Money was always tight, and the matter of an unidentified corpse who had not been claimed by any distraught family members, did not warrant a speedier response from his department.

"No other identifying items?" he asked.

Sophie shook her head. "The body was found in the nude, sir. However, there were a number of tattoos still visible, and I'm told by the pathologist that he's been able to photograph several quite clearly, which he'll send through to us in due course for comparison with Missing Persons. I've already completed a first run against the database, and have produced a short list of potential matches we'll be going through by process of elimination today."

He nodded, and gestured for her to continue.

"There was, of course, one clear identifying marker on the body, which is this carved image of a fish," she said, and tapped a knuckle against the photograph she'd tacked to the board. "We believe this was done either ante or post-mortem, and, as you can see from its position on the underside of the upper forearm, it would have been awkward for the victim to have done this to himself."

"You refer to him as a 'victim'," Pearce interjected. "You're classifying this as a suspicious death then, Sergeant?"

The main Criminal Investigation Department for the Cornwall and Devonshire Constabulary was based out of Bodmin Headquarters, which was an hour's drive away in good traffic conditions. At the insistence of her DCS, the Deputy Chief Constable had appointed Sophie as the Senior Investigating Officer on the case. It was a pragmatic choice, and she was a competent person to lead the investigation. It would have been an enormous professional opportunity, had she not spent every waking moment wondering whether her supposition was correct, and it was, indeed, her father who was responsible for the man's death.

LJ ROSS

To acknowledge her suspicion would also require an acknowledgement of her connection to the killer, which would likely mean professional suicide.

It was a quandary, and she knew she must make a decision by the time the body was identified.

"—Keane?"

She became conscious that the DCS still awaited an answer to his question, and hastily pulled herself together.

"Yes, I'm classifying the death as 'suspicious'," she said. "Aside from what looks like a ritual carving, it's clear the skin from each of the man's fingertips was removed prior to immersion in the water, sir. Added to which, it seems his legs were bound at the ankles, which is something the pathologist will confirm."

"Are you thinking there may be a gangland connection?"

"Yes," she said, clearing her throat. "We're investigating that angle, sir, but he doesn't belong to any known groups in our neck of the woods."

"Further afield, then? I'm told even hardened criminals take holidays."

Cop humour, she thought, *was the very worst kind of humour.*

"After a localised search of the vicinity, we did recover a pair of khaki walking trousers," she said. "We can't be sure they belonged to the deceased, but we'll send them for analysis and see if they throw up any leads."

"Any helpful witnesses?"

"That depends on your definition of 'helpful', sir," she said, with a smile. "We've had a lot of people volunteering information with very little bearing on the case and, since every report must be followed up, it's slowing us down."

She spared a thought for PC Turner, whose job it had been to wade through the telephone messages and statements given during the house-to-house calls they'd made the previous day.

"PC Turner has been doing a stellar job managing that side of things," she said, and he sat up a little straighter in his chair, flushing with pride.

Pearce was uninterested, viewing the admin of a case to be a necessary cog in the bigger wheel, and not worthy of any special attention. "Nobody's made a report?" he queried instead. "Nobody's missing their husband or father?"

His mention of the latter caused her stomach to dip, leaving her feeling sick with fear that he, Turner, and everyone else she'd come to know as an extended professional family, would turn their backs on her if they only knew...

"Nobody's been in to file a Missing Persons report," she said. "That doesn't mean somebody isn't missing him."

Pearce nodded, and checked the time on his watch, which was an expensive chunk of silver and gold his wife had given him for their last anniversary.

"Speaking of missing things, has there been any word on that painting?"

Sophie was surprised at the sudden change in direction, but answered him without pause.

"We believe the painting was stolen early on Wednesday morning, before the gallery opening on Thursday," she said. "Hardly anyone was around at the time, only the manager of the gallery, a woman by the name of Ingrid Roper, who'd let herself in just after eight to begin preparations for the opening the next day. She says that, when she arrived, the painting was still there. However, she popped out twenty minutes later to run and get a coffee from The Canary, and, by the time she returned at around eight-forty, the painting had gone."

"Are Roper's movements accounted for?"

Sophie nodded. "We checked her timeline, sir. The Canary is the only café-bakery open before nine, so there were plenty of people milling around who've confirmed they saw Ms Roper arrive and leave at the times she stated, takeaway cup in hand. The owner of the café has confirmed it, too, and her arrival time at the gallery was captured by on-site CCTV footage."

"Didn't the cameras capture the *thief*, for goodness' sake?" Pearce asked.

"The cameras are linked to the wider security system," Sophie explained. "It's brand new, very fancy, and ultimately not as effective as old-fashioned methods. The system has various 'modes', which include filming while the security system is turned on; filming when the security system is off; and not filming at all. To enable filming while the security alarm is turned off, you have to select the correct mode. Unfortunately, Ms Roper selected 'OFF' mode when she left to pick up her coffee, which means the cameras were turned off the entire time she was away."

"Sounds like she had a hand in things," Pearce said.

"We conducted a full search of Ms Roper's home, which was something she consented to without our needing to apply for a search warrant," Sophie pointed out. "Ingrid Roper is an experienced art dealer who has managed the opening of several of Luke Malone's galleries across Cornwall and Devon, sir. She is well remunerated, and has been in contact with pieces of far greater value than the one that was stolen. All things considered, it doesn't make sense for her to have been the perpetrator, but it is possible she was an unwitting player in the theft by virtue of being a creature of habit."

"I don't follow," Pearce remarked. "You're saying she helped without meaning to help?"

Sophie nodded. "It's possible the thief learned Ms Roper's habits over the past few days, which have generally tended towards getting a coffee around half past eight and returning ten minutes later. It's a short window to get in and out, but it can be done."

"It's one thing to get in and take the painting, but it's another to run through the streets with a painting that size," Turner piped up. "Where did they put it? A getaway car?"

Sophie folded her arms and considered the question.

"The only other people who were around at that time of the morning were the occasional jogger, a few dog walkers, of course, some trade delivery people and the waste collection team whose usual round takes them to the gallery's commercial bins at around eight forty-five. There's no parking at the gallery—you have to use the nearest public or off-street parking, as with most of the other businesses in that part of town," she said. "A car parked up anywhere on the wharf at that hour would have stood out, and been remembered by someone, and the same goes for the back entrance to the gallery on Fore Street. Either access is quite public."

"You think they made off with it on foot, or perhaps had an accomplice waiting nearby to help carry it?"

Sophie smiled. "Once again, I think our thief might have had an entirely unwitting accomplice," she said. "I think the binmen might have lent a hand, which is why I've been in touch with the waste collection service. There's a row of large, commercial dumpsters in the alley between the gallery and its neighbour, so it would've been the easiest thing in the world for someone to drop the painting in there as they left."

"Why would anyone want to steal a painting and then throw it away?" Turner asked. "It's hugely risky, for no gain whatsoever."

"That all depends on what you're hoping to gain," Sophie murmured. "If the idea is to re-sell the painting, then it would be difficult and the dividend wouldn't be high owing to the artist not being an established one, yet. However, if the idea is to destroy the painting, for some reason, then they've achieved their goal."

"I still don't understand why the painting was so offensive," Turner said, thoughtfully. "Why would anybody want to destroy it, if they weren't intending to sell it? It's just a picture of the bay at night."

"There's another possibility, which is that our thief—or thieves—could have been struck with last-minute jitters," Pearce pointed out. "Plenty of first-timers panic once they've committed their first theft, murder or whatever, and try to distance themselves from their own actions after the fact."

Sophie agreed it was a possibility. "That's true, sir, and I won't discount it," she said. "But, for now, I want to know more about the artist, Dean Mostend, and how, when and why he chose to paint *Moonlit Bay*. Perhaps he'll be the key to understanding why his work was stolen."

"Maybe there's something he isn't telling us," Turner said, getting excited about the prospect of some intrigue. "What if it's all a big publicity stunt, to help him make a name for himself?"

Sophie wondered if he'd been watching old episodes of *Miami Vice* again.

"That's certainly another possibility, and we'll keep it in mind," she said. "But, for now, I think our first port of call has to be Mr Mostend."

Pearce rubbed a hand over his face, stretched his arms above his head, and then stood up.

"Carry on, Sergeant," he said, and made for the door. "For God's sake, crack open a window—it smells like a hop house in here."

"That's my fault, sir," Turner said. "Had a bit of a heavy night, last night."

"Don't let it happen too often," Pearce warned him, and then, with a nod for the pair of them, disappeared back along the corridor.

In the silence that followed his departure, Sophie gave her constable one of her most fearsome glares, and pointed an accusatory finger at his chest.

"You don't need to cover for me like that, Turner. I smell just as bad as you do."

She paused, sniffed, and decided to amend her statement.

"Okay, I don't smell *quite* as bad as you do, but I'm at least partially culpable for the hoppy aroma in here."

Turner shrugged. "You're hard enough on yourself, Sarge," he said. "I don't want you to be put off the idea of ever going out again, just because you had one Pinot Grigio too many."

"Chablis," she corrected, automatically. "Not that it matters. Look, I appreciate the thought, but I'm always accountable for myself, Turner. It's a matter of principle."

And that, he supposed, was the mark of good leadership.

"C'mon," she said, rolling her shoulders. "Let's shake off the cobwebs, and pay Mr Mostend a visit."

"Will our route take us past The Canary?" he wondered aloud.

"Why? Do you need to ask some follow up questions?"

"No, but they might still have a couple of croissants left—"

"Move your arse, Turner."

"Yes, ma'am."

CHAPTER 13

"What's going on?"

A long line of parents and children ran along Fore Street, and Sophie's outburst was as much a reflection of confusion as to its source, as it was frustration that they were blocking entry to the bakery, where croissants awaited.

"It's leading all the way back to the bookshop," Turner said. "Who's here? JK Rowling?"

They saw children dressed in pirate fancy dress and other swashbuckling gear, many of them clutching dog-eared copies of books with bright covers to their chests.

"They're lucky it isn't raining," she murmured. "Hey, kid, who are you waiting for?"

A child of around ten or eleven showed her the book he held. It was entitled, *Ethan and the Smuggler's Chest* and its author was GS Rowe.

She might have known.

"I'm going to have my book signed by the author," he said excitedly.

His mother appeared less excited by the prospect of a long wait, but Sophie was fairly certain her outlook would change once she caught sight of the author himself.

"Isn't that Hot Date—?" Turner began, catching sight of a publicity poster in the window of the St Ives Bookseller.

"Yes," she interrupted, trying to compute the sheer number of people who'd turned out for him. Gabriel had been honest about his profession, but he certainly hadn't bothered to mention that he was clearly very good at it. "And it wasn't a *date*."

"Wow, look here," Turner said, ignoring her while he scanned through search results on his phone. "He's sold millions—"

"Stop stalking him," she said, as she peered over her constable's shoulder. "Wait, go back a minute."

Turner kept any smart comments to himself, and scrolled back to the previous page.

A moody, black-and-white photograph of Gabriel seated at a desk surrounded by hardback copies of his own books sprang from the screen, alongside a biography which told her that he'd sold at least ten million copies, that he lived in his native Cornwall but had attended Cambridge University where he'd studied English Literature. He'd worked as a journalist for a number of years in London, before publishing the first of fifteen novels ten years ago.

His books were being developed for the big screen, with the first film due to be released in time for Christmas.

Sophie didn't know how to feel about it all, and wondered why any of it should make a difference to her opinion of him, but it did. This morning, she thought she'd suffered enough embarrassment to last a lifetime, on top of the stress of hunting a killer who could very well turn out to be her own father. Now, to add insult to injury, the man who'd looked after her, washed her clothes, laid out aspirin and water, listened patiently while she'd hurled insults at him instead of thanks, and had even braved her dubious 'morning breath' to kiss her at the end of it all, wasn't just your average good-looking prodigal son come home to roost.

He was a *bestselling* one.

"Do you want to stop in and say 'hello'?" Turner asked, clearly champing at the bit. "I'm sure he'd let us jump the queue."

He wriggled his eyebrows, and Sophie would have laughed if she'd had the heart.

"We have work to do," she reminded him, and, much to Turner's disappointment, began striding away from the bookshop and its line of adoring fans.

"Should be up here, on the right."

Dean Mostend, the artist responsible for the fated painting *Moonlight Bay*, lived in a rented flat overlooking Porthmeor Beach. Less sheltered than the harbour and the other smaller beaches around the bay, it was open to the full force of wind and sea blowing in from the Atlantic, which made it popular with surfers looking to catch a wave.

"Bit blowy on this side of town, isn't it?" Turner remarked, and turned up the collar of the thin jacket he wore.

Sophie nodded, and looked up at the blue skies overhead. The sun might have been shining, but its rays were no match for the biting winds that rushed along the narrow streets, which formed a natural tunnel and almost blew them off their feet.

Presently, they came to a building constructed sometime during the seventies or eighties, which was a towering anachronism amongst the surrounding stone-built cottages. It comprised of three levels, each boasting four small apartments accessed from an external gallery that ran off a central concrete staircase, and its architecture reminded them both of an American roadside motel.

"We're looking for number five, on the second floor," she said, and they made their way up the stairs, dodging damp wetsuits and body boards as they went. "Apparently, he works out of the apartment rather than hiring a studio elsewhere."

Once they reached the western corner of the apartment building, they could understand why. The light from that direction was spectacular now that the sun had begun its westerly descent, and the views across the beach and out to sea were far-reaching.

They encountered no other residents during their progress, and they saw from the little plaques adorning the walls outside each passing door that over half of the apartments were holiday lets. Their visiting guests were probably out on the beach enjoying themselves and the fine weather.

"Here we are," Sophie said, as they approached a plain, blue-painted door. "Let's see if he's home."

After ringing the doorbell, and giving the wood a few hard knocks, it appeared he wasn't.

"That's a pity," Sophie said, and there was no handy window to peek through and double-check Mostend wasn't choosing solitude over social convention. "Hang on, I'll try the mobile number Luke gave me."

But the number rang out, and directed her to leave a voicemail.

"Mr Mostend, this is DS Keane, from Devon and Cornwall Police. We're hoping to have a word with you concerning the theft of your painting. If you could give me a call back on this number, or pop into the station, we can try to arrange a convenient time. Thank you."

"You've got a very polite telephone voice," Turner said, as they descended the stairwell again.

"Cold-calling," she said, flatly. "I had a part-time job ringing people up to see if they needed life insurance while I was at uni."

"Ironic, considering the job you do now," he was bound to say.

As they neared the base of the stairs, they ran into two teenagers of around fifteen or sixteen, who were clearly on their way to shower and change after a session in the surf.

"Hey, do you live here?" Turner asked.

"Stayin' for the summer," one of them replied, with the kind of sullenness typical of teens the world over. "Who's askin'?"

"DS Keane and PC Turner," he replied, and watched panic flit over their pimpled faces.

"We 'aven't done nothin' wrong," the other one said, clutching his surfboard like a lifeline. "We—"

"Calm down," Sophie told them. "We're not here for your bag of weed."

The pair of them cast telling glances in the direction of their holiday apartment.

"We only want to ask you whether you've seen much of the man living at Number 5?"

The shorter of the two boys shook his head, but the taller shrugged and nodded his assent. "Yeah, I've seen him a few times. Old bloke, around sixty? Always in the same gear, carryin' one of those wooden things painters have—"

"An easel?" Turner provided.

"Yeah, that's it."

"When was the last time you saw him?"

"Dunno," he replied. "We've been over at Beanie's place in Sennen for the past few days."

He referred to a larger surfing beach further along the coast. As for the aforementioned 'Beanie', it wasn't too much of a mental stretch to imagine a boy of around the same age with a penchant for wearing beanie hats.

"How about today?" Sophie prodded.

"Nah, not yet," he replied. "Look, is that it? I'm startin' to feel cold."

Indeed, the two boys were shivering badly now, the cold wind lashing against their wetsuits.

She let them go, then turned to her constable with a troubled frown. "We only want to question Mostend," she muttered, and reached inside her pocket for a crumpled brochure leftover from the gallery opening. Beneath the image of *Moonlit Bay* was a short biography of the artist which explained he was self-taught, and played up his natural eye for landscapes. "Do you think he's avoiding us?"

Turner shook his head. "Why would he need to?"

Sophie shook her head, which was starting to throb again. "The painting is less of a priority than the murder investigation, so let's focus on that."

"You used the 'm' word," Turner remarked, as they made their way back into town.

"I wasn't aware I'd called you a 'muppet' out loud."

He laughed, and shook his head. "Murder, is what you said."

Sophie smiled grimly. "So I did."

CHAPTER 14

Gabriel had been seated for more than two hours inside the bookshop, a ready smile on his face for each new child who approached him with starry eyes and a book in their hands.

I love your stories, Mr Rowe!

When's the next book coming out?

Gabriel's smile never faltered, though his hand began to cramp and his neck ached. He remembered being a child, once, and if he could provide some fertile ground for fantasy and escape from the realities of life through his adventure stories, then he considered it a privilege. A few aches and pains were nothing in comparison.

Can I have a picture with you, Mr Rowe?

The muscles in his cheeks were beginning to ache, too, but he worked them into another smile and held out an arm to a child of eight, who grinned into the camera her mother held up.

"Thank you," the woman said. "This has made her year!"

"Where did you get the idea for Ethan's character?" the girl asked, shyly.

It wasn't the first time a child had asked him that question, but he treated each time as if it was the first time, so that child was made to feel special.

"That's a great question," he said. "I suppose the character is based a little bit on myself, when I was a kid your age, and maybe a little bit on my father, who grew up around here as well."

"Cool," she replied. "Do you think Ethan'll ever track down the Mystery Men?"

She spoke of the band of nefarious smugglers and knaves he'd imagined on the pages, his young protagonist's constant nemesis, as Moriarty was to Sherlock Holmes.

"He's getting closer all the time," Gabriel said, with another smile. "What do you think he should do, when he finds out their true identity?"

The child thought about it, her face screwing up in concentration. "Well, Ethan's always fighting for what's right," she reasoned. "He wouldn't want bad things to happen to them, he only wants justice, so he should turn them in to the police."

Gabriel nodded gravely. "I'll keep that in mind, Annie. Is there anything else you'd like to ask me, while I'm here?"

"No, but when I grow up, I want to be a writer just like you."

"Don't be just like me," he said, with a gentle smile. "Be even *better*."

———

Sophie watched the exchange from her position at the back of the little bookshop, where she'd flouted her own better judgment and slipped inside as the tail end of the queue approached their literary hero.

"He's great with the kids, isn't he?" the manager said quietly. "Every one of them has left on Cloud Nine."

Sophie could only nod her agreement, but there was a tremulous feeling in her belly, the kind of nerves she might have experienced standing on the precipice of something very high.

"We've been trying to get him to come along and do a signing for years," the manager continued. "We were so delighted when he finally said 'yes'."

Sophie frowned at that, and wondered whether painful childhood memories were the only thing that had kept him away.

Gabriel stood up then, stretched out the kinks in his back, and then turned to see her standing there. His smile was automatic, and lit up his whole face.

"Hello Detective," he said, and walked towards her. "This is an unexpected pleasure. Would you like me to sign something for you?"

An old song from the eighties filtered through her mind, something about the object of the crooner's affection signing their name across her heart, and Sophie was mortified by the level to which her own psyche had obviously stooped.

Love songs?

Get a grip, Sophie.

"Actually, I stopped in to pick up a book for my mother," she lied, with the ease and long experience that came from play-acting a role for twenty-five years. "I didn't realise your signing was today, but we walked past the queue earlier—"

"Who's 'we'?" Gabriel asked.

"Me and my constable, Alex Turner."

Gabriel experienced a brief and totally unexpected explosion of jealousy at the thought of her spending her working days with a man that wasn't himself.

It was something to think about.

"Where's your constable now?"

She'd sent him packing, with instructions to chase up the pathologist and forensics team for any useful titbits they could work with to kickstart their investigation. Meanwhile, her next stop would be tracing the source of the only tangible piece of evidence they'd found, aside from the body itself: the walking trousers. It wasn't much, but it was all they had.

"Turner's making some enquiries," she said. "I only stopped in to ask whether you'd seen Dean Mostend on your travels? I think you said you were interested in buying the painting that was stolen, so I wondered whether you'd happened to see him? I thought, perhaps, you might have enquired about a commission, or something like that."

Gabriel looked away and raised a hand to brush the hair from his forehead. Her eyes followed the action before snapping back to the small notebook she held in her hand.

"I've seen Dean out and about with his easel," he said. "I've exchanged a few words with him, but not in the past couple of days. I haven't seen him at any of his usual spots, come to think of it."

He hadn't been at home when I called, either, he might have added.

Sophie's skin began to crawl, a slow, creeping feeling of a discovery she could not yet prove, but knew to be true.

"When was the last time you saw him, and where?"

"Why do you ask?" Gabriel said. "Is he under suspicion?"

No, Sophie thought. *She already had her prime suspect in mind, wherever he was.*

The only person left unidentified was their victim.

"I'd just like to speak with him," she replied, avoiding his question as much as he was avoiding hers.

Gabriel folded his arms across his chest. "The last time I saw him must have been Wednesday morning, the day before the gallery opening. He was painting out on the wharf, and I was out jogging. I stopped, and said, 'Good morning'."

Wednesday morning, she thought. *The same day the painting went missing.*

"What time would you say this was?"

"I couldn't say for sure—I don't work usual nine-to-five hours, so my frame of reference is different to most. Maybe seven-thirty or so?"

Her heart sank, for it fell within the timescale they were investigating.

"Did your route take you past Luke Malone's new gallery?"

"Of course," he said. The building was right on the front of the wharf, as she was well aware. "Look, where's this all going?"

She didn't answer him, but glanced around to check the shop was still quiet and their conversation would remain confidential. "Did you see anyone else hanging around the gallery at that time?" she asked. "Any parked cars or people loitering?"

He tried to remember. "I can't be sure," he admitted. He'd had things on his mind, and wasn't paying attention to much else. "I'm sure there were a couple of delivery vans parked here and there, dropping off food and drinks to the restaurants before opening. There might have been a couple of people walking dogs, too, but I didn't recognise them."

"But you stopped to speak to Dean Mostend?"

Gabriel nodded. "As I said, I saw him sitting on his little camp stool with his easel overlooking the water," he replied. "We exchanged a few words, that was all."

"How did he seem to you? Was he worried about anything?"

A couple of seconds ticked by while they stood there, each weighing up the other.

"No," he replied, at length. "I don't think he was worried. He was looking forward to the gallery opening, and hoped his painting would attract a buyer. I told him I would be interested, and he said I should speak to Luke, which I agreed to do. Neither of us could have known the painting would be stolen that very day."

Sophie listened to him, scribbled something down and then slipped her notebook back in her pocket.

"Thanks," she said. "I have to ask these routine questions, to build up an accurate picture of events."

"I understand. Did you want to pick up that book for your mother?"

"What book?"

The corners of his mouth tugged into a smile. "The reason you stopped in here—remember?"

"Right," she muttered, and turned around, scanning the shop with a desperate eye, then strode across to the crime fiction section. Thankfully, one of her favourite authors was on display, the book cover showing an atmospheric image of one of the most iconic beauty spots in the North East of England.

"This one," she said, snatching it up. "Mum loves these murder mysteries."

It happened to be true; in fact, they both enjoyed the series, partly because its setting reminded them of their old homeland.

Gabriel glanced at the cover of the book, which featured a castle against the backdrop of a beautiful sky, and then nodded.

"Have you ever been to Northumberland, Sophie?"

It was an open question, she reminded herself. He couldn't possibly know it was the place where she was born.

"Yes," she replied, with a casual nod. "Lovely part of the world, isn't it?"

He nodded again, interested by the sudden change in the tone of her voice. "These stories feature a detective—DCI Ryan, if I remember correctly?—who suffers a tragedy and takes himself off to a tidal island in the first book, to escape from the world and give himself time to recover. Have the stresses of the job ever driven you to St Michael's Mount?"

"Not yet," she admitted. "But there's still time."

She moved to the cash desk, where the bookseller rang up her purchase. Gabriel waited until she'd finished, made his own round of thanks and farewells, then held the door for her to precede him as they stepped back outside into the early afternoon sunshine.

"Would you like to go for a walk?" he asked her.

Sophie thought of all the work still to do, but a short walk couldn't hurt and she was due a break in any case.

"All right," she said. "Where shall we go?"

"Let's start by getting an ice cream," he said, with a flash of boyishness she was growing to like so much. "How long can you spare me?"

Not long enough, her heart whispered. "Ten or fifteen minutes," she said aloud. "We can eat our ice creams on the way back to the police station, if you don't mind walking in that direction."

"I'll take whatever I can get."

"Easily pleased, aren't you?"

Gabriel gave a little shake of his head and thought that, *no,* he wasn't usually. He was a man accustomed to running his own life, dancing to his own tune—and it hadn't been *Cotton Eye Joe.* He'd come to St Ives for a very specific reason, or perhaps better to call it a *mission,* no part of which included a woman with deep, dark eyes whose depths were fathoms deep and filled with untold secrets.

It complicated matters.

CHAPTER 15

"I can't believe you snuck back to the bookshop without me."

"There was no sneaking involved," Sophie said, with dignity.

From his position at the desk opposite hers, Turner stuck his head around the side of his computer monitor and made a sound like a raspberry.

"You did, too—and don't think I didn't see you, chomping on that ice-cream cone as if it was—"

"Don't you dare say it!"

"—your last meal?" he offered, with a lascivious glint in his eye.

"You know," she mused. "When I was a young constable on the road to becoming detective, I'm sure I showed my senior officers a lot more respect."

"Your senior officers weren't stepping out with Henry Cavill's younger, better-looking brother. It changes things."

"Get your mind out of the gutter and tell me how the pathologist is getting on."

Turner leaned back in his chair and switched back into professional mode. "The short answer is that he isn't making any progress, really. He's apologetic, but he's snowed under with bodies at the moment—"

"There's an image," she muttered.

"—and he doesn't think he'll get around to our DB until Monday. He's working overtime as it is."

She nodded. "I suppose I'm wasting my breath asking whether we've had any word from Scenes of Crime?"

"Same story, boss, although they've promised to get onto it as soon as possible."

How 'soon' was 'soon'? Sophie thought, and took a long gulp of lukewarm tea.

"I've got a couple of minor developments, although they don't feel like much," she said. "The first is that I finished going through the list of potential missing persons in the area, and none of them are a physical match to the body we recovered. DNA comparison would confirm it, in some borderline cases, but my gut is telling me none of them are a match."

She'd never been wrong before.

"Once forensics are able to extract a DNA sample, we can run that through the system and see if anything flags on the register."

Turner nodded. "What was the other development?"

"No luck tracing the trousers we found, but I'm going to try the shops again tomorrow, when some of their staff have rotated," she said. "The only other development was that I heard from the waste management company in the case of the missing painting. They've confirmed their men did the rounds at eight-thirty on Wednesday morning, and the waste taken from the dumpsters beside the gallery was transported to a site near St Austell."

She referred to a town around an hour's drive away.

"I've asked a couple of bobbies from the Bodmin office to go over there first thing on Monday to see if the painting can be found," she said. "The waste management company have agreed to try to filter some of the rubbish to help us out."

She glanced at the clock on the wall, which told her it was five-to-one.

"Why don't you go and grab some lunch, Alex? There's nothing more to be done here, for the moment, and I'll stay and listen out for any calls."

"Well, if you're sure?" he said, already reaching for his sunglasses. "Call me, if anything turns up."

She waited until he'd left the room and then, in the privacy of her own company, allowed her shoulders to sag and her smile to slip.

It had been a long couple of days, and the investigation was only just warming up.

Earlier in the day, she'd put some private calls through to charities that specialised in helping former prisoners re-integrate into the community, but none of them had a 'Michael Gallagher' listed on their books. Likewise, it was the same story when she spoke with local hostels and B&Bs in the area surrounding HMP Frankland, as well as those located off the motorways and dual carriageways that connected the North with the South of England. The problem was there were too many potential variables, which would take considerable time to explore; for instance, had her father squirreled away any money over the years? Or, had he made friends on the inside who could help him start a new life outside the system? It seemed likely, given his track record. If he had means, that changed everything, for it meant that he could purchase or borrow a car and drive himself down to Cornwall, which made it more difficult to trace his movements than if he'd taken a bus or a train.

Her next logical place to check was hospitals.

It hadn't escaped her attention that he'd been released on compassionate grounds, and a deep dive into the limited press coverage following his release told her that he'd been diagnosed with a brain tumour that was inoperable and, according to the specialists, terminal.

Sudden tears blurred her vision, and she pushed away from her desk to stand and pace around, scrubbing the offending leakage from her eyes.

He didn't *deserve* her tears.

But, she realised, they weren't for the Mick Gallagher the world knew. They were for a Mick Gallagher who'd never existed, except in her four-year-old imagination. He was nothing but a childish figment, a collection of memories comprising snapshots of experiences that showed only the best corner of his personality and not the rest, which belonged to a brutal gangland killer.

As soon as she was old enough to understand about her father, at around eight or nine, her mind had instantly begun to imagine scenarios where the police, the jurors and everyone else was mistaken. In her broken heart, she imagined him a wronged man, an innocent person who'd become embroiled in a criminal world against his will. There must have been some sort of duress, some logical reason why her father had been mistaken for another man.

But there was no mistake.

Her teenage years had been particularly difficult, as she'd ridden wave after wave of hatred and frustration, devastation and anger towards her father. The first time she'd ever broken the rules had been when she was sixteen, old enough to search for and find the case reference number needed to contact Frankland and try to arrange a visit to see him. She had no real plan, no idea of how she'd get there without her mother finding out, but she needed to look into his eyes and ask him the one, burning question she'd longed to ask for most of her young life…

Why?

Unfortunately—or fortunately, depending on the point of view—the question became moot, because Mick Gallagher hadn't wanted to see his daughter and refused a visit. The incident became the first as well as the last time she'd ever reached out to the man who'd fathered her.

Since he wasn't around, nor available to speak to in any capacity, the young Sophie had only one outlet left…

Her mother.

It was Kim Gallagher or, rather, Jacqui Keane, who'd borne the brunt of her daughter's rage. She alone had weathered the storm of tears and reprisals, hurt and accusations, until Sophie had purged herself. She hadn't turned to drugs, thank goodness, and had only briefly experimented with alcohol with a tribe of other kids her age. Boys weren't a problem; if anything, Kim worried her daughter would never be able to trust a man and that, of all his heinous actions, Gallagher's parting gift to his only child would be a lasting inability to love and be loved in return.

Sophie caught her own reflection in the window, which looked out across a concrete car park, but she saw nothing of the view. By the time PC Turner returned, two takeaway coffees in hand, he found his boss sitting comfortably at her desk, looking very much in command of herself and others as she worked her way through a list of regional hospitals, beginning with the Royal Cornwall Hospital in Truro.

One way or another, she always got her man.

CHAPTER 16

Derek Tailor liked to think he was a 'man of the people'.

In truth, he wasn't entirely sure what it meant to be a man of the people, but he'd heard it often enough, and likeability was highly desirable in his line of work, so he was happy to go along with it. Besides, he could always tone down the working-class origin story, if the company demanded it; some of his higher-end clients didn't like to feel discomfited by things like class divides in society when they were thinking about buying a fourth or fifth property, or a super-yacht.

Another thing Derek Tailor liked to think was that he was a *self-made man*, and, for the past forty years, he'd said it often enough that people believed it to be true. In reality, as with many 'overnight success' stories, he'd had plenty of help along the way, which enabled him to get on the ladder and to flip his first few properties, all of which had been sold for a considerable profit. He'd always had an eye for pretty things, whether they be houses, pieces of jewellery or people.

The prettiest of them all, in his opinion, was Wharf House. It was unrivalled in its location, its architecture and design were superlative, but its greatest selling point for him was its unattainability. The house had been in the Rowe family for generations, and he'd coveted it since the very first time he'd ever walked inside its front door.

Come on in, Derek, and have some supper!

If he closed his eyes, he could still remember the warmth that surrounded his skinny, malnourished body as he'd stepped over the threshold and into the home of his schoolfriend, John Rowe. He could see the comfortable chairs and smell the enticing scent of fish pie warming in the oven. It was a world so very different from his own, where his father had been laid off from more jobs than they could count, and his mother did her best with the meagre pickings that she had. He was loved, but he had none of the trappings his friends could boast, and he *wanted* them.

He wanted *all* of them.

Now, as a man of sixty-five, he wanted Wharf House.

He'd *earned* it.

If he was truly honest with himself, he hadn't been a friend to John Rowe so much as a hanger-on, determined to ingratiate himself within a circle of friends whose situation in life was something to which he aspired. Spending time with their families, he began to learn certain social graces, and taught himself to speak with the King's English rather than his own Cornish dialect. He wanted to be able to travel anywhere and not be set apart; he wanted people to wonder where he came from and assume it was London, not a back alley in a Cornish town that served only to remind him of all the things he didn't have.

Now, as he stood a few feet from the entrance, he looked upon the façade of Wharf House and felt the same, terrible yearning he'd always felt. How could a family who'd merely inherited a house ever truly appreciate its value? It required a custodian; someone of note in the county...

Someone like himself.

Gabriel was on a roll when a knock came at the door.

He was tempted to ignore it and focus instead on the scene he was crafting, but he thought there was a chance it might be Sophie on the other side and so he roused himself to answer it.

He regretted his decision instantly.

"*Gabriel*, my boy!"

Though older, in spite of a liberal application of Botox, he recognised Derek Tailor almost immediately. Thirty years ago, he'd been another of his father's friends, though even as a boy he'd struggled to see what they could possibly have in common. Where John Rowe had been affable and kind, Derek Tailor had always seemed to him a grasping, greedy sort of person, never afraid to capitalise on even the smallest advantage that presented itself.

Which was, Gabriel suddenly realised, precisely why the man had come to call.

"Hello, Mr Tailor," he said. "Would you like to come in?"

Derek's eyes were already seeking out the interior, and he entered the house like a visiting sultan. "Nothing's changed, really," he said, mostly to himself. "A few upgrades, a lick of paint, and it would be a show home."

Gabriel folded his arms and leaned his long body against the wall. "I've always preferred a home to be a home," he said, looking around the living room with a fond eye and realising, then and there, why he'd never really settled into his house in Charlestown. He'd renovated it with the help of a design team, who'd delivered exactly the specification he'd asked them to, and yet he'd never felt at ease amongst the new furnishings and smart countertops.

They compared unfavourably to his real home, with its uneven walls and rustic beams.

"Of course you do," Derek said quickly, and gave a tinkling laugh that grated on the nerves. "It's been much too long since you came to see us, Gabe. You've been missed."

It was a lie, and they both knew it.

"I heard you'd come back with a view to selling the old place," Derek continued, and told himself to go gently, not to show his hand too early, but his upper lip was already sweating with the prospect of Wharf House one day being his.

"Did you?" Gabriel said. "I'm afraid whoever told you that is mistaken."

"Mistaken?" Derek repeated.

Gabriel nodded. "Wharf House isn't for sale."

Derek fell back on the principle that had made him a millionaire: never take 'no' for an answer. "Well, I hope you won't be offended by this, Gabe, but don't you think it would be better for the community if you let a nice family live here, rather than keeping it as a second home?"

He sank into one of the chairs, and prepared to dish out some home truths—no pun intended.

"When people hoover up housing for temporary use, they're depriving local people of the chance to buy because it drives house prices up so much that they can't afford to, even if they're given the chance," he said, blithely overlooking his own private property portfolio. "And all for what? To bring in a few bob as a holiday let?" He tutted. "I wouldn't have thought that's something you would want to do to the old place," he said, and then leaned forward to give his next message an air of authenticity. "Now, think of this: I could sell the place for you...of course, it's not brand new, and the kitchen and bathrooms probably need to be replaced, so you can't expect to achieve the *highest* price, especially in today's market."

He spread his hands.

"That being said, I've always had a soft spot for this place," he said, and was careful not to sound too enthusiastic. "I'd have to speak to Molly, and you know she's perfectly happy where we are, but—"

He paused, pretending to think about it, and then smiled at Gabriel.

"I could take it off your hands, and you'd have the peace of mind knowing we'd take good care of the old girl," he said, rubbing one slimy hand against the stonework. "Just say the word, and we can get the paperwork drawn up this very afternoon. You can go home with a lighter heart and a heavier wallet, and I'll make sure Wharf House is returned to its former glory."

Already, he could visualise the voice-activated lighting system and the mirrored bathroom ceiling. Gabriel saw all of it and more behind the other man's eyes, and thought he'd spent enough of his precious time listening to emotional blackmail from someone whose interest was only ever to acquire, and then acquire some more.

"Thank you for the offer," he said. "However, as I've already told you, the house is not for sale and that's my final word on the matter. Now, if you'll excuse me, I'm afraid I have a lot of work to do and I'm already well behind on my deadline."

He moved towards the door and held it open.

Tailor kept a smile fixed on his face and held it there until long after the door shut behind him. It stayed there as he walked swiftly along the wharf and remained there until he reached his car, which was parked in the station car park.

Only then did he allow the mask to slip and, when it did, it was as though a waxwork figure had melted in the heat of the afternoon sun.

"Never take 'no' for an answer," he said to himself. "Or simply create the conditions for them to say 'yes'."

If Gabriel Rowe wouldn't sell of his own accord, perhaps it was time somebody showed him how uncomfortable life at Wharf House could really be.

CHAPTER 17

After the interlude with Derek Tailor, Gabriel was unable to settle back into his story and so took himself off for a walk. He wandered the streets of St Ives for more than an hour, stopping here and there to pick up a coffee or sit and watch the waves on the far side of the Island. Every curve and corner of the place held a memory for him and, if he'd expected to find the weight of it oppressive, he was pleasantly surprised to find that it brought a sense of belonging. For the first time in many years, he was reminded that he was part of a community and, if he chose to, he could put down roots and let them grow. Perhaps he would, if it were not for the fact that he knew a killer lived amongst that sleepy community, breathing the same air, walking the same streets, and feeling the same sand between their toes.

He didn't know their name yet, nor even their motive for killing his father, but he knew it as surely as he knew his own face.

One of them had murdered John Rowe.

Anger welled up again as he thought of that unknown person continuing to live and prosper, while his father had died and been left to rot in a windswept cemetery. His reputation as a drunkard had been forever emblazoned in the minds of those who remained, his many years of service as a general practitioner long forgotten by all but his son and perhaps a few kind-hearted souls with longer memories than most, and it wasn't right.

Lost in these troubling thoughts, Gabriel hardly realised he'd come to a place known as 'Island Square', which was accessed from the wharf by a road known simply as Back Road East. It connected St Ives harbour to the other side of the island peninsula, and led to Porthmeor and Porthgwidden beaches respectively. On the little square was a charming café and a couple of shops, one of which appeared to sell locally-made candles and other smelly bath stuff, though their wares were marketed with considerably more finesse than that.

Scents of Cornwall, the sign read, in pretty, pale-blue lettering.

He wondered what his home county smelled of, really, aside from sea and salt, sand, fresh air and earth, but perhaps it was time to find out.

Jacqui looked up at the sound of the door jingling, which signalled the arrival of a new customer. Since she was neither blind nor mute, honesty compelled her to admit that he was one of the best-looking men she'd ever seen and, if she'd been twenty years younger, or he twenty years older, she'd have closed the shop early and thrown caution to the winds.

You tried that once before—remember?

The voice inside her head belonged to her younger self, and she was reminded of the terrible consequences of being drawn in by a handsome face and a kind smile. They could be deceptive.

Gabriel discerned none of these thoughts from the face of an attractive, fifty-something lady behind the counter, and he returned her welcoming smile with one of his own.

"Hello," she said, with just a hint of a residual Northern twang. "Are you looking for anything in particular?"

Gabriel looked exactly as he felt, which was completely out of his depth.

"Um," he said, eloquently. "There's this woman I know. She has a stressful job, I think, and I saw your shop, so I thought…I don't know."

He trailed off, looking confused and surprised by his own inclination.

"How thoughtful," Jacqui said, warmly. "If your friend has a stressful day job, perhaps she might like to unwind at night, maybe with some calming bath salts? These are locally made, and contain lavender and sage, a little bit of lemongrass and a few other things—"

She reached for a tester pot and held it out for him to sniff.

"Nice," he remarked.

"A man of few words," Jacqui said, with a chuckle. "How about this one?"

As they sniffed their way around the room, Gabriel began to feel light-headed.

"The first one," he said eventually. "Although, I think my nose failed me after the sixth tester pot."

"It can be a bit overpowering, to an untrained nose," she laughed. "Would you like me to package this up, or would you consider a gift set?"

She reached for a smart white box containing several products in the same range.

"I can wrap this for you in a ribbon of your choice," she said. "I call this blend, *St Ives Sunset*, and it happens to be my daughter's favourite."

Gabriel smiled and reached for his wallet, wondering when he'd morphed into the kind of man who bought toiletries for women he barely knew. "Oh, is your daughter in the bath salt business, too?"

She smiled and shook her head. "No, she's the sensible one," Jacqui replied, as she began wrapping up his purchase. "Sophie's a detective sergeant with the police force. She works out of the office here in St Ives, actually."

Gabriel's hand froze in the act of reaching for his wallet, then he smiled broadly. "You're Sophie's mum?"

Jacqui cocked her head. "You two know each other?"

The note of maternal interest was unmistakeable, and he began to worry he'd leapt straight out of the frying pan and into the fire.

"Well, it's always lovely to meet one of Sophie's new friends," Jacqui said, and waved away his wallet. "This one's on the house. The shop's quiet at the moment, so why don't I show you how the candles are made, and you can tell me all about how you know my daughter."

"I—" Gabriel made a strangled sound of panic, but could think of no plausible reason to decline her offer. "Thanks."

She indicated her 'potion counter', where she made candles and wax melts. "Come on," she said, wickedly. "Let's see if those hands can do more than type."

He looked at her in surprise. "You recognise me?"

"Sweetie, I run the town's foremost book club, and you were our pin-up for three consecutive months."

"I—" He was utterly lost for words, and she patted his hand in a maternal fashion.

"Best not to think about it," she advised. "Now, what about these jugs?"

"*What*?"

She held up a glass jug and a porcelain one. "Which one would you like to use?"

"Oh," he said, with some relief. "I'll take either."

"Not fussy, eh? Well, that's no bad thing."

Blissfully unaware that her mother was, at that very moment, showing Gabriel a selection of pictures of herself at various awkward ages—including her personal favourite 'denim-on-denim' selection from the early-noughties album—some sixth sense nonetheless guided Sophie in the direction of her mother's shop, where she intended to call in and have the dreaded conversation about Mick Gallagher that could wait no longer.

The light mellowed as she made her way along Fore Street and then up the back roads towards Island Square, and the sun which had been strong at the height of the day was now thinning to a gentle swathe of amber light which fell over the town. It was hard to believe that, amid such beauty, there existed what some might have called evil; but then, she'd seen plenty of it to know that it could exist anywhere.

When she arrived at Island Square, she was surprised to find Scents of Cornwall bearing a 'CLOSED' sign, and checked the time on her watch.

Four-thirty.

On Saturdays during the high season, her mother tended to keep the shop open until at least five-thirty to afford visiting tourists every opportunity to make their souvenir purchases, and also to allow many a local man the chance to run in and make a last-minute anniversary purchase for their beloved, to go alongside a card from the stand she kept beside the till.

Jacqui Keane was a businesswoman *first*, and a romantic *last*.

Or so she always claimed.

Sophie peered through the glass window and almost rubbed her eyes, to be sure they weren't deceiving her. It looked very much as though Gabriel Rowe, world-famous children's author, was standing at her mother's potion counter stirring lavender into a large mixing cauldron, laughing at something she'd just said. Feeling oddly voyeuristic, Sophie almost took to her heels to make a swift getaway, but hesitated and lost the opportunity, for they turned then and saw her peering at them both.

"Sophie!" Her mother gave an excited wave and hurried over to unlock the shop door. "Come in! We were just talking about you," she said, drawing her in for a warm embrace. "I've been showing Gabriel how to make candles."

"So I see," Sophie said, meeting his eyes over the waxy cauldron. "It seems you move like the Scarlet Pimpernel. You're here, there, and everywhere."

He held up his gloved hands in a sign of mute appeal. "It's a fair cop," he joked. "Despite my own better judgment, I've enjoyed every minute of this impromptu candle-making class. Thank you, Jacqui."

"My pleasure," she said and, to Sophie's amazement, patted his cheek as though she'd known him for years. "Remember to leave plenty time to let them set, if you're planning to make any at home."

It would be a cold day in hell before he found the time to make his own candles, but he appreciated the thought.

"I'll just wash my hands, then I'll leave you both to it," he said, sensing correctly that Sophie was hoping to have some time with her mother alone.

As he walked towards the staff cloakroom, Jacqui turned to her with a face that was positively giddy with maternal excitement. "He's a lovely young man." She classified anyone below the age of sixty as 'young', nowadays. "So well-mannered—"

"Why is he here?" Sophie hissed.

"Why do you think?" Jacqui said, as if it should be obvious even to a simpleton. "To buy a present for you."

"Me? *Why*?"

Jacqui looked into her daughter's eyes and realised that she was still so *young*. It seemed improbable that her strong, independent daughter should be fearful of something so natural, but then, she hadn't made it easy for her. After Mick's behaviour, she'd blamed herself for having been so blind and foolish, and she'd wanted to caution her daughter to be wise. It occurred to her that, maybe, she'd gone too far, and it was time to repair some of the damage.

"Perhaps he was thinking of you, darling?" she said.

"I barely know the man!"

"And you're going to have so much fun *getting* to know one another," she said, and gave her a meaningful nudge.

Sophie's eyes widened just in time to see Gabriel walking back into the main shop.

"Is there anything I can help with?" he asked, innocently enough.

"I'm perfectly fine, dear, but I'm sure Sophie can think of something," Jacqui murmured.

Gabriel looked between them.

"Well, you know where you can find me," he said, and then lowered his voice so that only Sophie would hear him. "I often work late at night, Detective. Come and knock on my door, if you feel like some company."

Sophie's body responded before her brain could and, when it did, her imagination went into overdrive. "This is moving too quickly," she muttered.

"I agree."

"I don't trust you," she said bluntly.

"I don't blame you," he shot back. "And, just for the record, I don't trust you either."

She frowned at him. "I'm a *police officer*," she argued.

"So what?"

They stood there for a silent charged moment, until he stepped away, retrieved the white gift bag her mother held out to him, and reached for the door handle.

"I'll see you later, Detective," he said, and made her feel hot all over again. "Jacqui? Thanks again for a great tutorial."

He stepped out into the balmy summer night, and they watched him stroll back across the square and disappear around the corner of one of the stone cottages on the far side.

"See? The parcel wasn't for me," Sophie said, after a few moments. "He took it away with him."

Jacqui merely smiled. "You know best, sweetheart."

CHAPTER 18

"You're sure it's the same as before?"

Sophie watched her mother battle shock and disbelief as she stood by the window in her kitchen, and was sorry to have been the cause of it.

"I'm as sure as I can be," she said quietly. "I've compared the photographs taken of the knife markings on the body we found the other day with the images on file relating to his…to Michael Gallagher's victims back in the nineties. They're almost identical."

It was easier to refer to him by his full name, she'd discovered. That way, she could almost forget he was family.

"It could be a coincidence," her mother said, desperately. "Or—what do you call it?—one of those copycat killers?"

Sophie said nothing, but her silence spoke volumes.

"You think he's the killer," Jacqui concluded, and her shoulders sagged. "But, *why*? Why would he come here and kill somebody?"

"I need to find the answer to that question," Sophie said. "It had all the markers of a professional gangland murder and, as soon as I discover the identity of the victim, things will be a lot easier for me to piece together. Whoever killed him removed any obvious identifying factors, which only leaves DNA identification, and there's a risk he isn't listed on the database—not everybody is."

Jacqui turned to face her daughter. "If Mick's down here roaming the area, we have to leave—"

The old fear and loathing reared up, as potent as ever.

"No," Sophie said, very calmly. "We won't be going anywhere, Mum."

Jacqui searched her daughter's face. "He's dangerous," she whispered. "I don't want you to be hurt, or the life you've built to be spoiled. Not again…not after all these years."

A single tear escaped, and she turned to scrub the plates in the sink, keeping her face averted.

Sophie picked up a tea towel and crossed the room to put an arm around her mother's shoulders.

"He can't hurt us now," she said, and hoped it was true.

Jacqui shook her head, miserably. "Even after all this time, he still has the power to—to—"

"He has *no* power," Sophie interjected. "He's older, he's dying, and he isn't dealing with a young woman and a small child anymore. He's dealing with you, a successful businesswoman with life experience, and with *me*. I represent the long arm of the law, and I won't hesitate to use it."

She turned and began drying the freshly-washed dishes with deliberate strokes.

"I won't argue that Gallagher isn't still dangerous," she admitted, after a few quiet moments had passed.

"But if he knows we're here and wanted to harm either of us, he'd have done it by now."

Jacqui shivered, despite the warm weather. "What—what will you do, if you find him?"

Sophie turned and looked her mother dead in the eye.

"*When* I find him, he will be given the same treatment as any other suspect in a murder investigation," she said. "I'll read him his rights, before bringing him in."

Jacqui felt fresh tears well up, but they were all for the little girl she'd once known.

"You shouldn't have to do this," she whispered. "It's not right—"

"It's my job," Sophie said, and left it at that.

It's my job.

Sophie replayed her own words as she let herself out of her mother's house an hour later, and waited until she heard the comforting *click* of a lock being bolted behind her before heading off.

It was her job, but the question was—for how long?

If her suspicions were correct, then the time was fast approaching for her to hold a meeting with DCS Pearce and come clean about her familial connection with their prime suspect. She'd been holding out for something, *anything*, to point her enquiry in another direction but, so far, no other alternative had presented itself. The time was drawing near when she'd need to muster the courage and the words to say what needed to be said—and soon.

But, as soon as she did, Sophie knew that nothing would ever be the same again. She would no longer be DS Sophie Keane, trusted member of the community and rising star of the Devon and Cornwall Police. She would be an impostor, a confidence trickster, and the reason for her deception was unlikely to elicit much in the way of sympathy.

She began walking, her footsteps echoing around the quiet back road while she visualised herself sitting in the cramped, airless vacuum of DCS Pearce's office, laying bare her family history while he made murmuring noises of understanding. She could imagine the gossip machine whirring, spreading all the sordid corners of her life far and wide to be picked over by people like Jenna Pearce or Molly Tailor.

The apple never falls far from the tree, they'd say.

Bad blood, just like her father.

Not to be trusted…

And they were right. How could they trust a woman who'd lied to them for almost thirty years? She'd lived in St Ives as one of their number, adopted as their own, and wore a uniform designed to instil confidence.

She was nothing but a hypocrite.

Tears blurred her vision and her footsteps quickened. Instead of heading to her own modern apartment overlooking Porthminster Beach, she made for the wharf and the house that stood there like a silent sentinel, watching them all for more than two hundred years.

If only its walls could talk.

———————

Gabriel looked up at the sound of a quiet knock at the front door and set aside the book he was reading to pad across the room and greet his visitor.

"Hello again," he said.

Before she could talk herself out of it, Sophie stepped inside and let the warmth of the house seep through her cold bones before taking stock of her surroundings. Gabriel was dressed simply in blue jeans and a white shirt, leaving his tanned feet bare against the rug, and he was, at that moment, watching her with one of his lazy, knowing smiles. A book lay discarded on the overstuffed couch across the room, and the lights were mellow against the velvety darkness outside, the last of the sun having left them hours before.

"For a wordsmith, you're very economical," she said.

"Would you rather I quoted Shakespeare, or Shelley?" he asked, and leaned back against the front door while she paced around his living room. "Or, how about: *Whenever I'm alone with you, you make me feel like I am home again?*"

Sophie felt something spread in her chest, like the wings of a bird. "The Cure," she said softly. "You like The Cure?"

"Doesn't everybody?"

"Everybody who's sane," she agreed, and then swallowed as he pushed away from the door and moved towards her slowly, like a jungle cat.

"Would you like something to drink? To eat?"

She shook her head and he paused, never crowding her, giving her all the time in the world to tell him what she *did* want.

"We hardly know each other," she said.

"Mad, isn't it?" he replied. "I really should be more careful—you could be anybody."

His words were too close to the bone, and served to remind her that she wasn't in the market to begin a relationship. She barely knew who she was, having played a role for so long. How could she expect anybody to love her?

"I'm not looking for anything serious," she said bluntly, but the words didn't ring as true as they once had.

He took another careful step forward, and reached out to touch her hand.

"What *are* you looking for?"

She found herself looking up into eyes that were a luminous blue, and very open, willing her to be open in return.

Love, laughter, a happy family, she wanted to say.

"Escape," she replied, keeping her tone light.

Gabriel frowned. "I'll still be here in the morning, Sophie," he said. "I know about personal demons, and what it's like not to sleep for days. It wears you down until you're not sure who you are anymore."

Her eyes welled up, but she didn't cry.

"Escape is fleeting," he continued. "And, eventually, there comes a time when you realise you can never escape yourself."

He took her face in his hands and spoke softly to her.

"Maybe, at one time in my life, I'd have been happy to be your escape," he said. "But not any more. You say you're not interested in anything serious? I suppose I'll have to try and change your mind about that, won't I?"

Before she could respond, he leaned down and brushed her lips with the gentlest of kisses.

"I'm not going anywhere," he muttered, before drawing back again. "I've decided to stay in St Ives, not just temporarily but for as long as I'm happy here. There's time to get to know one another, if you give it a chance, Sophie."

As far as rejections went, it was the kindest and most flattering she'd ever received, and—damn the man—made her want him all the more.

"Why don't we watch a movie together?"

Before she had time to feel embarrassed or upset, he surprised her all over again.

"I can go home—"

"Why? We could both use the company, and I'll even let you choose the film."

"What if I choose something like *Sleepless in Seattle* or *You've Got Mail*?"

"Are you kidding? I love both of those," he said, and passed her the remote. "I'm not adverse to *One Fine Day* or *French Kiss,* either, but I prefer *A Fish Called Wanda.*"

"You like Monty Python?"

"Technically, that wasn't a Monty Python film, but yes, I'm a fan," he called back, on his way to the kitchen for snacks and drinks.

Left alone in the cosy space, Sophie found she was smiling again. It was not how she'd envisioned the night progressing, not by any stretch, but it was exactly what she needed. She appeared to have found the rarest of unicorns: an intelligent, good-looking man with a successful career, who had enough moral fibre to turn down her unspoken offer because he sensed her vulnerability—even when she would have overlooked it—in favour of being her friend, first. There was enough chemistry between them to spark an explosion and, on top of it all, they shared a similar taste in music and films. He was even good with children and mothers— and, in the case of her mother, that was no mean feat.

Where was the catch? she wondered.

There was always a catch.

While Sophie and Gabriel debated the merits and demerits of films made in the nineties, two men gathered in the shadows, protected by the sound of the waves crashing against the sea wall and the opaque darkness that surrounded them like a shroud.

"He knows," the taller man said, casting his eye around the vicinity for any moving shadows.

"He doesn't know anything," the other replied. "He can't possibly know."

"I'm telling you, he *knows*. Why else would he come back here, after so long?"

"To see the old place again, sign a few books, and enjoy himself with our lovely local sergeant, it would appear."

That was news to his friend.

"That's *all* we need," he hissed. "Bad enough Gabriel's back again, asking questions and raking up the past, but to involve—"

"Calm yourself," came the firm reply. "And keep your voice down, for God's sake. He was—what? Ten or eleven when it happened. He may be older now, but the story is the same. He was a kid who thought he heard voices...so what? People sympathise, they nod and smile, but he couldn't tell anybody what he thought he heard, couldn't give any useful details or even identify the other voice. He could only say he thought his father was arguing with someone on the night he died."

He laughed softly.

"Easy enough to imagine John raving at someone or another, given the state he was in. Most people probably thought the kid overheard his dad raving at his own shadow."

Guilt pricked at the other man's heart. John Rowe might have been drunk that night, but he'd been clear-sighted enough to notice what was happening beneath his very nose.

His mistake had been in confronting them about it.

"If he'd just kept his trap shut," he muttered. "Nothing would have happened."

"If wishes were horses," came the bored reply. "We can't bring him back and neither can Gabriel. It's time he let this go, or—"

He lifted a shoulder.

"No—surely, there's no need for that—"

"Let's hope Gabriel has more wit than his father—he may live longer."

CHAPTER 19

In her dream, Sophie was drowning.

Her arms and legs struggled against the almighty wrath of the sea, but her weight was no match against the gallons of salty water that came to bear, dragging her further and further down into its murky depths with unseen hands.

No—

No!

"Sophie!" Gabriel said, having been rudely awakened from their uncomfortable sleeping position on the sofa in his living room. "Sophie, wake up!"

But she couldn't hear him, only the garbled sound of a man's voice calling to her somewhere from the deep. Her chest rose and fell rapidly as she dragged air into her sleeping lungs, and beneath the water her chest screamed, and her legs kicked out with desperate strokes as she continued to fight the inevitable.

Gabriel held her shoulders in gentle hands, in case she was to fall from the sofa and hurt herself.

"*Sophie!*"

In the dream, she heard her name again, and through the tangle of seaweed that curled itself around her ankles, she thought she saw a figure.

Suddenly, Mick Gallagher's face materialised, grey and eerie, his eyes staring through her.

Daddy! her mind cried. *Daddy, why aren't you helping me?*

Sophie screamed, fighting the hands that held her, believing them to be malevolent. Gabriel held on as carefully as he could, shifting himself to block her body from falling, with an eye for the chunky oak coffee table that was perilously close to her head.

"Sophie? It's me, Gabriel! Wake up, Sophie!"

He'd experienced a few night terrors himself in his time, but never anything so severe as to prevent him from regaining consciousness. Various ideas presented themselves, from cold water to a firmer shake of the shoulders but, in the end, he decided to hold her steady until her mind was ready to return to him.

Eventually, her body went lax, the fight seeming to drain from her, and he tried again.

"Sophie," he repeated. "Wake up, Sophie. You're safe."

Her eyes flew open and, when they did, they were wide with remembered terror. Her pupils were dilated, her skin pale and clammy, and it took her a moment to remember where she was, and with whom.

"What happened?" she whispered, scrubbing a hand over her face before dragging herself into a seated position.

"You had a terrible nightmare," he said, feeling shaken by it himself. "I couldn't wake you."

"Oh," she muttered, and dabbed away the sweat that caked her brow and the back of her neck. "It's been a little while since I've had one of those. Sorry," she tagged on.

"For what?" he asked, and took a seat beside her.

She gave a self-conscious shrug. "We've only known each other for a few days, but it seems that you're constantly having to look after me," she said, and was mortified about it. "I'm not usually such a liability. Normally, I'm the one—"

She thought of her mother, her friends, the people of Cornwall.

"—to look after others?" he finished quietly.

When she didn't reply, he reached across the back of the sofa to run a comforting hand over her hair. "I know you can be strong," he said quietly. "I've seen how you hold yourself together, how you shoulder what you must have seen the other morning to be able to lead the investigation. You can't wear the mask all the time though; none of us is superhuman."

"You got all that from knowing me less than three days?"

"Writers are very observant," he pointed out. "For instance, I'd say you're also very *secretive*, which makes me want to know more about you."

The shutters came down again, and he was fascinated to watch it happen.

"There isn't much more to know," she said.

"Liar," he whispered.

Sudden tears burned the back of her throat, and he was instantly contrite.

"I'm sorry, I—"

She shook her head and reached for a tissue to blow her nose—loudly, much to his amusement.

"What was that? I didn't catch it over the sound of that foghorn."

She gave him a playful shove, and they looked at one another for a long moment. Then, he held out an arm, beckoning her to lean in.

Slowly, she rested her head against the solid wall of his chest.

He had a strong heartbeat, and she listened to it for a few moments while her body continued to recover, enjoying the secure feel of his arm around her shoulders and the even rise and fall of his chest. The television had reverted to 'standby' mode somewhere in the middle of *Kindergarten Cop* but the side lights still burned a dim, comforting glow. They heard nothing outside, except the incessant lap of the waves against the harbour wall, and the distant thrum of music being played somewhere in the little township.

"You give good hugs," she mumbled. "What time is it?"

He raised a free hand to check his watch.

"Two o'clock," he said. "We must've fallen asleep around midnight."

"It's late," she said, and started to move away.

He tugged her back, and she didn't put up much of a fight.

"It's late," he agreed, and rubbed the side of his cheek against the top of her head absentmindedly. "Why not stay here? I have a guest room, as you know. In fact, I was thinking of putting a plaque on the door with your name on it."

Sophie managed a smile but thought, very clearly, that she had no desire to be in the guest room. Before she could say as much, his next question caught her off-guard.

"Do you want to tell me about your dream?"

Usually, she awakened alone in her own bedroom, feeling lost. The thought of having someone to talk to was unexpected, and intoxicating.

"In my dream, I was drowning," she began, her voice muffled against his shirt. "I couldn't breathe, couldn't see anything but the water and it was cold...so *cold*. There was no light, and I couldn't find my way to the surface—"

She shivered, and he held her tighter, rubbing his hand over her arm both to warm her and remind her she was no longer there in the darkest corner of her own mind.

"Someone was there, in the water," she continued, her voice barely audible as she grasped at the threads of her memory. "I'm not sure who it was."

"You called out 'Daddy' several times," he said gently. Although she'd never mentioned it, he had already made the assumption that she'd lost her father, as he had, because the empathy she'd shown towards him seemed to come from her own lived experience and was hard to simulate.

"Did I?" She sat up, putting some distance between them while her mind battled with her heart.

Eventually, the latter won, as it often did.

"I've never spoken of this to anyone," she said, fixing her gaze on the empty television so she wouldn't have to see the disappointment on Gabriel's face, once he found out who she really was. "Not my friends or work colleagues, or anyone else aside from my mother. I don't know why I'm telling you, now…perhaps because you're still an outsider, or maybe it's something about the way you listen so intently. You make me feel heard."

Gabriel leaned forward, wanting to touch her, but sensing it wasn't the time.

"Grief is a private thing," he said, thinking of his own. "It isn't something that's easily understood by others, unless they've experienced it themselves—"

Her lips twisted, and she thought of all the dark, guilty times she'd wondered if it would have been better if her father had died.

"I've grieved, but not in the way that you mean," she said. "Gabriel, you won't like me anymore after you hear what I have to say. You won't want to sit and watch films and laugh with me, or have anything more to do with me. I know that, but I have to tell you anyway, or I'll go mad. I'm tired of hiding it."

He frowned. "Sophie, what's this about? Losing a parent isn't something I would ever ostracise anyone for; in fact, I'd be the last person to—"

She stood up then, running agitated hands through her hair, wondering where to begin.

"We aren't the same. My father isn't dead," she said, although, technically speaking, she didn't know where Michael Gallagher was. "My mother and I lost my father the day we found out he was a killer, and things were never the same again."

There was a stillness to the house, and, to her fevered mind, it seemed that the walls expanded and contracted in shocked reaction to her outburst.

Gabriel continued to watch her with an expression of kind understanding.

"Did—didn't you hear me?" she demanded. "I just said my father is a killer. A *murderer*. He took another person's life, probably many others I don't know about, and I'm *part* of him. He made me, and I look a bit like him, as well."

Gabriel thought he'd given a good impression of a soul in torment in his time, but he realised he'd met his match in Sophie.

He stood up and walked across the room to take both of her hands in his own.

"No, don't touch me."

"Why? Do you think I'll catch something? Behaviour isn't contagious, Sophie. You know better than I do, from the people you see each day, that we are each the masters of our own destiny. Okay, sometimes circumstances—opportunities or a lack of them—can steer the direction of a person's life, but fundamentally the choice as to how we act in any given moment is still *ours*. You aren't responsible for the actions of your father."

She'd told herself the same thing many times before—her mother had, too—but it was easier to say it than to believe it.

"You said you hadn't told anyone about your father," he continued. "How long have you lived with this?"

She looked down at the hands he continued to hold.

"Twenty-five years," she said. "We went into the Witness Protection Scheme. My real surname isn't Keane."

He thought of her mother, who'd seemed the essence of a confident older woman, successful and full of vivacity despite everything she must have lived through. He would never have guessed the reason she'd moved to St Ives, nor that her daughter bore such a heavy cross each day.

The human spirit was an incredible thing.

"You'll want some time to think about this," Sophie was saying. "I understand that, so I'll be on my way."

She stepped back and tried to smile.

"What is there to think about?"

She huffed out a sigh. "Gabriel, don't play games with me. Can't you see, I'm trying to give you a way out, and leave with a scrap of dignity intact?" Tears threatened, but she shoved them away. "I love this town and the people in it, but I'm not blind to their faults," she said. "I've seen the gossip mill churn somebody up over an extra-marital affair or an unpaid parking fine—"

"People are people, the world over," he agreed. "I've seen the worst that a small town can bring. I lived through the whispers about my father, 'The Drunk', and far worse after he passed away. I'm no stranger to it, Soph, and I know how damaging words can be."

She nodded, enjoying the accidental abbreviation of her name coming from his lips.

"Then you'll know how merciless they'll be," she said. "They'll feel betrayed. I don't worry so much for myself, but I think of my mother, and the effort she's made to be part of this community."

Gabriel knew that Jacqui sat on the trustee boards of several small charities, and was often seen doing a charity fun run on the weekends, or dropping packages off to the needy after hours. Hers was a giving, forgiving nature, and she'd passed much of that onto her daughter.

"I understand," he said. "I won't pretend there aren't a few bigoted people hereabouts, as you'd find in any town the world over, but I also know there are more good people than bad in this world. For every one person who'd look askance, there'd be another ten who'd think of the hardship you and your mother suffered in being separated from all you knew, and blamed for the decisions your father took with his life. It's clear to any thinking person that you love this town, and you do your best every day to serve it, and the wider county of Cornwall. Nobody can do more than that."

When she struggled to find any words in response, he took her hands again, and she didn't tug them away this time.

"If you need somebody to stand in your corner, I'll do it, Detective, and gladly. But I know there will be others, if it ever becomes necessary for you to tell people."

It was becoming more necessary by the day, she thought.

"I've met the victims of crime," she whispered. "I've delivered the worst news, and been a shoulder to cry on. I've seen the devastation, Gabriel, and it's heart-breaking. It turns my stomach to think that I'm related to someone who could inflict that kind of pain and suffering. I can't expect anybody to forgive me; not in those circumstances."

A shadow passed over his face and, this time, he was the one to step back.

"There would be nothing to forgive you for," he said, not meeting her eyes. "It's the perpetrator of a crime who faces the judgment of the community."

There was a tone in his voice that made her wary, something she couldn't put her finger on but found concerning.

Her eye fell on the book he'd been reading hours before.

The Count of Monte Cristo.

Funny, she thought. 'Edmond Dantes' was almost an anagram of 'Dean Mostend'.

He was still missing.

CHAPTER 20

The next day

The *Outdoor Clothing Emporium* did exactly what it said on the tin.

Sophie thought this as she pushed through its double doors alongside PC Turner, armed with an evidence bag and a prayer.

"It's still a long shot that anybody will remember who bought these trousers, but it's worth doing another circuit of the clothing stores since there aren't that many," she said.

Turner nodded, and polished off the last of his croissant.

"I don't know how you're so slim," she muttered. "Your veins must be made of iron."

"It's the muscle memory," he said, tapping one skinny bicep. "That's why I burn off the fat so quickly."

"I don't remember you having any muscles," she said, doubtfully. "Are you sure it isn't worms?"

"I had the memory of a muscle, once," he said, with a grin.

She shook her head, and they made their way towards the cash desk.

"Hi, Janet," she said, recognising the owner of the shop. "Thanks for your time, yesterday. I think you said a couple of staff would be changing over today. Is it possible to have a word with the changeover staff, please?"

Janet Duggan was a friend of her mother's, but Sophie was long past feeling any awkwardness in discharging her duty amongst the people of St Ives. She'd grown up with so many of them, it would be a futile effort.

"Of course, my lamb. I'll be back in a jiffy."

Terms of endearment were also permitted, in limited number.

Presently, Janet returned with a young woman in tow, whom she introduced as Alissa, and who turned out to be nineteen and working there for the summer before returning to Falmouth University in the autumn.

"Hi Alissa," Sophie said, and retrieved her warrant card to let her see it. "I don't know how much Janet has told you, but we're investigating a murder. I don't want you to worry, there's no suggestion you're in any kind of trouble, we're only here to ask some questions that could assist us in our enquiries. Is that okay?"

The young woman nodded but looked awestruck by it all, which was a common reaction from people who'd never had any interaction with the police before.

"We understand five pairs of these walking trouser have been sold in the past couple of months, all in khaki green, men's size large," Sophie began. "We've already traced three of them using digital receipts kept on record here in the shop, but the remaining two belong to people who preferred a paper receipt—"

"Ooh, just a sec, I spent some time last night trawling through our records here, and I've found the other two receipts," Janet put in, and Sophie could have kissed her.

"Janet, if you ever fancy coming to work for me as an intelligence analyst, just let me know."

The older woman laughed and waved it away. "I turned down MI6 in the late seventies, you know," she said, in the same cheery tone, before wandering off to see to a customer, leaving them all gaping after her.

"Always the quiet ones," Turner muttered.

Sophie glanced over the receipts, noting the dates on each of them and whether anything else had been purchased alongside the trousers.

One of them was a single purchase, the other, dated four weeks prior, also included a black raincoat.

"All right," she said, and showed Alissa the receipts. "Let's take this one, first. The purchase is only for a pair of these trousers, and was made on this date. Do you remember that day, Alissa? It was a..." Sophie paused to check her phone calendar. "It was a Thursday, and the till register says it was made at ten-fourteen a.m."

The girl tried to cast her mind back, but it was a struggle.

"Honestly, I can't remember," she said, pulling a face. "If they just pick something up from the rack and bring it over here to pay, it's harder to remember individual purchasers because they all kind of blend in together..."

Sophie understood, but the frustration was real.

"Okay, how about this one? This customer also purchased an all-weather jacket in men's size large," she said. "The purchase was made first thing on a Saturday morning—"

"Oh, hang on a second," Alissa said, and the words came out with a slight lisp owing to the new tongue piercing she'd treated herself to. "I think

I might remember this one. Yeah, yeah, I think he was waiting for us to open, because he was the first customer of the day. I don't remember the trousers in particular, but I remember the jacket because he really wanted that one from North Face, and we didn't have his size on the peg. I had to go to the stock room and find one for him."

Good enough, Sophie thought.

"That's great," she said. "Can you describe the customer to me, Alissa? Was he young or old?"

"Kinda old," she said, bluntly.

"What age range are we talking about?" Sophie enquired, having learned the hard way that, at a stately twenty-nine, she was already considered over the hill by a great number of the local youth population.

"I dunno," Alissa said, and screwed up her face, which was heavily made up and sporting the longest pair of false eyelashes they'd ever seen. "Maybe my grandad's age, so about fifty or sixty?"

Sophie began to get the 'tingle'.

"How about his skin tone, what colour was it?"

"Oh, he was white, with balding grey hair," Alissa said, without hesitation. "I can't remember what colour eyes he had, or anything like that, but he had tattoos on his arms, I remember that because he was wearing a t-shirt when he came in."

"Is there anything else you could tell us about him? You're doing really well," Turner added, with an encouraging smile.

"Um, yeah, I remember he was carrying some sort of folding wooden thing around with him," she said, looking up as she tried to picture him again. "He kinda smelled funny, like a petrol station."

"Could it have been turpentine?" Sophie murmured.

"I'm not sure what that smells like," Alissa said.

"Never mind. Do you remember anything else at all? Did he chat about anything, mention anything?"

"Oh, yeah, he was going on about some art thing he was part of," came the reply. "He said he had a painting that'd pay for the jacket and a lot more, if his boat came in."

"If his boat came in?" Sophie repeated.

"Yeah, then he started humming some tune and left."

Sophie nodded, fiddled on her phone for a moment to try to find a picture of the artist Dean Mostend, and found to her surprise that there was no image of him on the gallery website.

Unusual.

Likewise, a Google search brought nothing.

"Thank you, Alissa, you've been very helpful."

The girl looked pleased with herself but, as they turned to leave, she seemed to remember the reason they'd come to her in the first place.

"Hey—is the old man going to be all right? Is he in trouble or something?"

Sophie thought of the body that now lay on a cold metal slab at the county mortuary, and forced a smile onto her face.

"He isn't in any trouble, now," she said, and turned to leave.

Outside, they paused in the shade of the shop's canopy while Sophie considered where to go next.

"We need to speak to Luke Malone and his gallery manager, Ingrid Roper," she said. "C'mon, Turner, shake a leg."

"Why?" he asked.

"Because you walk too slowly."

"No, I mean, why do we need to speak to the gallery again?"

Sophie reminded herself that he was still learning, and it was unreasonable to expect him to join the dots as quickly as she did.

"Who do you think Alissa just described in there, Alex?"

"An artist of some kind—*oh*."

"There it is," she muttered, and carried on walking.

"But why would anybody want to kill Dean Mostend?"

"Why steal his painting?" she countered. "We're on the trail now, Alex."

CHAPTER 21

The harbour in St Ives consisted of three piers—Smeaton's Pier, West Pier and New Pier—with two small lighthouses on Smeaton's, which happened to have been built adjacent to Wharf House and had, amongst other things, been the site of John Rowe's tragic end.

It was a busy harbour, accommodating a fleet of boats for hand line mackerel fishing, leisure and passenger boats and other hire craft comprising over a hundred moorings. Much like The Sloop, it had a long history, having been the largest port in the area in the mid-fourteenth century, boasting its own weekly market during the fifteenth century and a reputation as the chief port of western departure to Ireland by the sixteenth. Smeaton's Pier had been built a couple of hundred years later, and was intended to be used as a breakwater to intercept the strong, longshore currents from entering the harbour. The harbour master was overseer of all comings and goings, and the first person to speak to about everything from mooring a boat to tracing a missing vessel, stocking up on ice supplies and learning about water safety. His office stood at the entrance to Smeaton's Pier looking out to open sea in an easterly direction towards Godrevy lighthouse, four miles further inland, and its harbourside wall backed on to Wharf House, making Tom Cutter, the harbour master, one of Gabriel's closest neighbours.

"Thought you could use a coffee."

Cutter looked up from his inspection of an advance weather warning to find Gabriel framed in the doorway of his office, a couple of takeaway cups in hand.

"You thought right," he said, and smiled his thanks. "Haven't had time for my usual cuppa, this mornin'."

"Been busy?"

"Non-stop," Cutter replied, leaning back in his chair to roll out his neck and back, which still ached from the previous day. "Lines were all messed up t'other night, after the storm. It's been a devil of a job to put 'em right."

Gabriel thought of the lines connecting each boat mooring, many of which were in constant use during the season.

"Need a hand?"

Cutter raised a bushy grey eyebrow. "Kept up with it, then?"

Gabriel nodded. "I take a boat out once or twice a month, around Charlestown and thereabouts," he said, but the truth was that he was highly proficient, thanks to a lifetime spent learning not to hate the water that robbed him of the man who'd first taught him to love it.

"John always had a way with it," Cutter said, reading his mind. "If you've a mind to go out again, I can organise a loan for you."

Gabriel nodded his thanks, and took a sip of his coffee.

"Look, Tom, I'm here because I want to find out more about my father," he said. "I want to hear stories about him from the good days—before he lost my mother. I want to know the man better, even though he isn't with us, anymore."

Cutter took a long drink of coffee, and set it down again, studying the man standing before him. "Will it do any good?" he asked. "Will it help you to set 'im free?"

Gabriel smiled. "I'm sure of it."

Cutter nodded slowly. "In that case, I'll have a word with Arthur—Harry and Derek, too, since they knew 'im as well as any of us. About time we gave John the proper send off, and it's only right you're there with us, lad."

Gabriel raised his coffee in a toast. "Name the time and place, and I'll be there."

Cutter watched him leave, then stood up to study the progress of a couple of kayaks paddling their way between the harbour and the neighbouring bay at Porthminster, then reached for the mobile phone inside his pocket to make the calls.

———

The new art gallery was bustling by the time Sophie and Alex arrived, a combination of locals and tourists looking to purchase something to remind them of a happy trip to Cornwall. A quick call to her friend, Luke—the gallery owner—had ensured his prompt arrival within half an hour, and he was already waiting to greet the pair of them by the time they stepped inside.

"Hello, Sophie, Alex," he said. "Are you in need of a drink?"

Turner opened his mouth to accept, but Sophie intercepted his fifth coffee break of the morning with one of her warning stares.

"We're fine, Luke," she said. "Thanks for making the time to see us."

"Happy to help," he said, and indicated they should follow him to the office, where Ingrid was already waiting.

When they stepped inside, they found an unexpected fifth.

"Madge!"

A beautiful golden retriever looked up from her position atop an enormous dog cushion, gave a 'woof' that sounded incredibly like 'hello', and wagged her way across the room to nuzzle Sophie's hand.

"I haven't seen her in ages," she murmured and, all thoughts of police duty forgotten, she crouched down to give the dog a proper snuggle while Turner looked on in amazement.

"I thought you were a cat person," he said.

"Cats, dogs…any animal that has a kind soul," she corrected him. "A limited number of humans included."

Sophie stood up again, with regret.

"Has she put on a bit of weight since the last time I saw her?" she asked. "I could swear you've been feeding her too many pasties, Luke."

He grinned, gave his dog an affectionate rub behind the ears, and then let her settle back on the cushion after she'd taken the time to give Turner's crotch a thorough sniff.

"I changed my trousers today," he protested, at her indignant sneeze.

"She can smell last Friday's exploits a mile off," Sophie pointed out.

"Her sense of smell will be especially sensitive at the moment," Luke said. "She's expecting."

Sophie grinned, and almost gave the dog her congratulations before remembering they couldn't talk.

"That's wonderful," she said.

"Well, let's just say, *unexpected*," Luke said, and gave Madge the side-eye. "One day, a handsome pedigree Labrador came to stay at one of the holiday cottages in Carnance, and managed to seduce this lady from her loving home for a wild night on the beach. I didn't think she had it in her."

"She does now," Turner said, and four other heads turned to look at him with varying degrees of distaste. He held up his hands in mute appeal. "No offence!"

"Madge is a *lady*," Sophie enunciated, very clearly. "If she was led astray, it was most likely by some sweet-talking up-country dog who gave her some long-winded story about moving to the area. Isn't that right?"

The dog gave a nod of her elegant head.

"The cad," Luke chuckled. "Probably won't pay puppy support, either. Anyway, enough about the dog's turbulent love life. I suppose you've already met Ingrid, my manager?"

They shook hands again.

"I'm sorry, Detective, but I haven't been able to remember anything else about the theft," Ingrid began. "I've been racking my brain for something I missed—"

Sophie held up a hand.

"I appreciate that," she said. "Actually, we're here on another matter."

"Please, have a seat."

Sophie and Alex took up the visitors' chairs and, as soon as their posteriors hit the surface, could only liken the sensation to having landed on a cushioned cloud.

"Oh, God, we need these for the office," she burst out. "I'm usually numb by two o'clock."

"No way would the DCS stump up for anything this nice," Turner muttered. "It's all we could do to get some air freshener for the gents."

"On which delightful note, I'll turn to matters in hand," Sophie said. "We aren't here about the stolen painting, this time, but in regards to our investigation into the murder of a man found on Porthgwidden beach the other morning."

Ingrid nodded, and her hand crept up to her neck.

"Awful," she said. "We heard about it from Mrs Pearce—"

Sophie and Alex exchanged a knowing look.

"I see. Well, it's public knowledge now," she said. "However, we still haven't identified the body, and we're having some difficulty in doing so. Earlier today, we took some clothing that washed up nearby and traced its potential source to one of the local outlets here in St Ives. One of the sales assistants there was able to give us an accurate description of the buyer, who matches the physical description of Dean Mostend."

Luke and Ingrid wore twin expressions of surprise, then sadness.

"Wait a minute," he said. "You're saying you believe the victim was *Dean*?"

Sophie nodded. "It's looking to be a strong possibility, although we're awaiting the results of forensic testing to confirm," she said. "In the meantime, we don't have much else to go on aside from what you can tell us about him. I can't seem to find a picture of him anywhere, for instance, and I never met the man personally, although I've seen him a few times from a distance sitting on the pier beside his easel."

"He's only been in St Ives for a month or so," Luke pointed out. "He came with several canvases already completed, and *Moonlit Bay* was his last work which he finished only recently—it was his best, in my opinion."

"I asked him to come in to have his picture taken for the catalogue several times," Ingrid recalled. "He was very reticent and kept putting me off, until it was too late, and we needed to send the catalogue to print."

"I wonder why he wouldn't want his picture taken," Sophie said. "Was there any obvious reason?"

Luke shook his head. "He was presentable; a low-key dresser but always clean and tidy," he said. "He was...well, I suppose he looked like a lot of men around his age. He was an average height, with thinning grey hair he kept short on top, and he usually had a bit of stubble he fashioned into a goatee. He had a couple of tattoos on his arms, but they were old ones, I'd say, and he usually kept them covered. There was nothing that should have made him camera shy, anyway."

THE BAY

"If anything, he was an attractive older man," Ingrid admitted. "He kept himself in shape."

"Do you know anything else about his background?" she asked. "Does he have any family? I couldn't find any social media presence online, no website or old article written about him, which is remarkable."

Luke and Ingrid looked at one another, then shook their heads.

"He was very old fashioned," Ingrid said, and her use of the past tense wasn't lost on any of them. "He didn't want to have any social media accounts, because he said they were a waste of time—"

"He wasn't wrong," Luke put in.

"I tend to agree, but it might have been helpful to us, in this case," Sophie said.

"He didn't mention having any family—" Luke began.

"No, I think he mentioned having an ex-wife," Ingrid put in. "I'm sure he said he hadn't been the best of husbands to her, but he was hoping to

242

make amends one day. I thought it was a noble goal."

"He didn't give a name or an address?"

"Nothing like that, no."

"I suppose it's pointless for me to ask whether he happened to mention the name of someone who was out to get him?" Sophie asked.

It was a moment's levity.

"No such luck," Luke told her. "Honestly, we hardly knew the man. He only came in once before the gallery opened. Most of our business was conducted over the phone, beforehand."

"How did you discover him?" Turner asked.

"It would be better to say that he discovered us," Luke replied. "He rang me one day and turned up to my gallery in Truro, armed with an almost-complete *Moonlit Bay* and another armful of smaller canvasses. I thought he had something, and he was eager to start making money from his work."

"Did you ask about his personal history?"

Luke nodded. "Of course, but I didn't give him the Spanish Inquisition—there was no reason to. He told me from the outset he had no formal training, only a lifetime's worth of trial and error. There's a lot of saleability in that kind of story of raw talent, so the fact he didn't come to me with a degree from St Martin's was no bad thing. He told me he'd travelled the world, but had decided to settle in Cornwall for a while."

"He had a slight accent, come to think of it," Ingrid said. "I'm not sure if it was Irish—"

"It wasn't," Luke said, being the only authority on the matter considering he was an Irishman born and bred. "I think he had a slight Northern twang."

Sophie looked up at that, then back down at her notebook.

"The tattoos," she said. "Do you remember what they were?"

"One might have been a bird," Ingrid mused, and then shook her head. "Nope, I'm sorry, I just can't remember."

Luke shook his head as well. "I never saw them."

Sophie brought up an image on her phone, then prepared to ask a difficult question.

"I have an image of the body," she said. "It's of the man's face, but I have to tell you it's unpleasant viewing. You aren't obliged to look at it, at all, but I have to ask whether you'd be willing, to see if there is any similarity to the man you both met."

Ingrid looked panicked, but Luke stepped forward.

"Let's see," he said, and held out a hand to look at the screen.

His mouth tightened in response to the image presented to him, but he forced himself to look at the remains of a face with a critical eye.

"It could be him," he confirmed. "The line of the jaw, the nose...there isn't much left of whoever this was, but...yes, I think it could be Dean."

He handed the phone back to her, and then rubbed his hands together as if the image had transferred itself onto his fingers and made them dirty.

"I'm sorry I can't tell you more about him," Luke added. "We hadn't even taken bank details from him, or anything else that could be useful aside from his address, which you already have. That would have changed if he'd sold a painting or been offered a commission, but—"

"The only document we have is his signed contract with the gallery," Ingrid said and, with a few clicks, she brought up an electronic document. "He preferred a hard copy, so we have this one filed away in one of the drawers. It doesn't tell you anything more about his personal life or much else beyond his arrangements with the gallery here."

They spent a while longer asking everything they could think to ask, then asked their questions all over again, but when they emerged back into the early afternoon sunshine Sophie and her constable were left with the impression they'd spent the past hour or more discussing the past life of a dead man.

"What next, boss?"

Sophie looked up at the blue skies overhead, then down at the pavement beneath her feet.

There is no heaven, there is no hell, except here on Earth, she thought.

"We need a warrant to search Mostend's property," she said. "Make the call, Turner."

"Yes, ma'am."

CHAPTER 22

Mostend's apartment building was much the same as it had been the day before. This time, a crowd of surfers and sun-chasers gathered to watch the procession of four police personnel making their way up its central staircase, dressed in protective clothing and carrying a battering ram known affectionately in the ranks as 'the Enforcer', 'Sam' or sometimes 'Bosher'.

Amongst some of her staff, Sophie was also known as the Enforcer, though it was in large part owing to the fact she was considered small but mighty. She'd never allowed any disparity in physical strength to be determinative of her strength of command.

"Let's go," she said, and gave the order to enter.

A single heavy blow was sufficient, and Sophie was reminded all over again of a night long ago, when people just like herself had given the command to enter her parent's home and break apart the life she had known, piece by piece.

"Mr Mostend! Devon and Cornwall Police! We are entering your property!"

The warning was procedural only, for when they made their way along the tiny entrance corridor and into the main room of what had been Mostend's home, it was plain that nobody had been there for days. The smell of vegetables gone bad mingled with turpentine and oil-based paint was overpowering in the small space, and fruit flies circled a bowl of black bananas sitting on the counter of a tiny kitchenette.

"Crack open a window, before we all suffocate," she said, and Turner threw open one of the cheap u-PVC windows to allow some air to circulate.

They moved methodically, checking every cupboard and wardrobe, behind and underneath the single sofa and inside the cistern of the toilet in the bathroom for anything belonging to Dean Mostend, but it was as if the man had never existed. Not a single identifying document or personal effect was found, not even his toothbrush.

"What does that tell you, Turner?" she asked.

"He probably had terrible teeth?" the man offered. "Maybe they were taken out by a dentist rather than his killer, and we've been barking up the wrong tree."

"Ha ha," Sophie said. "It *tells* us that whoever killed Mostend got here before we did. They had his key, entered the property, removed all traces of the man as they did with his body, to make it all the harder for us to find his connections and the probable reason he was killed—"

She thought for a moment, looking around the room, and then down at the floor, which was a worn cream travertine tile, probably installed when the apartment was built. If she looked closely, she could see the faint line where a rug had once lain.

"Pull back," she murmured, and then repeated the order in a stronger voice. "Pull back! Deposit shoe coverings in an evidence bag by the door. This may be a kill scene."

Turner looked shocked, and jumped back with a rustle of plastic.

"Why do you think it happened *here*?"

Sophie pointed out the outline, then sniffed the air again.

"There's more to the smell here than turps and rotten fruit," she said. "There's bleach, and plenty of it."

Turner drew in the air, grimaced, and then nodded. "You're right."

"Now, go and put a call through to Irwin and tell him he's needed again. I want this entire place swabbed for blood spatter."

"If they used bleach, won't that have removed all traces?"

"It removes the blood so it's no longer visible to the naked eye," she said. "It's still possible to retrieve a DNA sample, but it can inhibit the detection, especially on smooth surfaces like tile flooring. It'll depend on whether the perp used a strong or weak concentrate of bleaching agent, for one thing."

"Let's hope they're not houseproud," Turner said, and made the call.

While he spoke with the forensics team, Sophie edged around the room and stepped out onto the small terrace area, which overlooked Porthmeor Beach and was the only square footage they hadn't searched. There was a bistro table with seating for two and, unseen from the apartment's interior, a drying rack upon which a wetsuit and a raincoat hung limply beside one another.

The jacket was black, made by the brand North Face, and was a men's size 'large'.

Sophie smiled, thinking of all the lovely DNA that would likely remain embedded in the fibres of both garments.

"Every contact leaves a trace," she said to herself.

It was two more hours before Sophie and Alex came to leave the apartment building, having sent the other constables packing to allow entry to Irwin and his assistant scenes of crime officer, who set to work on the area she indicated, first.

"DNA sampling from the other day should be with you by tomorrow," he said. "As for this, we'll turn it around as swiftly as we can, but you know there's always a backlog to deal with."

"But there isn't a backlog of active murder investigations in Cornwall," she said, having checked the current status of active cases herself, that morning. "We take priority over a non-suspicious death."

Irwin couldn't argue with that, and it was with a feeling of having won a small victory that Sophie made her way down the central staircase again, a feeling that was soon dispelled.

"Back again?"

This, from one of the two youths they'd questioned the previous day.

"You find 'im, then, or what?"

She smiled, but didn't answer.

"I'm glad we've run into one another again," she said. "I remember you telling us you'd seen Mr Mostend once or twice, is that correct?"

"The old bloke, yeah, we did."

"Did you happen to see anyone else with him, anyone who seemed threatening?"

The teenager shook his head, which was caked in sand and sea.

"I'm not sure if he was threatening, but you wanna speak to that tall feller."

"What 'tall feller'?" Turner snapped.

"The one on the posters," the kid snapped back. "His face is all over town. He writes books for little kids, or somethin'."

He'd enjoyed a lot of them, himself, but he wasn't about to say as much in front of his mates, who hung out of their apartment window watching the exchange.

Turner gave Sophie a quick concerned look, but her face was fixed and hard, like granite.

"You're talking about the author, Gabriel Rowe?"

The teenager bobbed his head. "Yeah, that's the one. He was round here, wasn't he? Came and went like a flash."

Sophie took down the details of his coming and going with a shaking hand.

"There's probably a good reason," Turner said, as soon as they were alone again. "Don't worry about it until there's a reason to."

It was a phrase she'd often said to him, and she was gratified to find he listened, but not moved enough to listen to it herself.

Gabriel had been there.

Had he killed?

Had he been the one to remove all traces, to slice away a man's fingertips and carve out his teeth, before dousing the place in bleach?

It was all too easy to imagine.

"Time to go," she muttered.

"To the station?"

"No," she said, in a voice carefully devoid of emotion. "To Wharf House. It looks like you're going to have an opportunity to meet Mr Rowe, after all, Alex."

This time, there was no funny rejoinder.

CHAPTER 23

Gabriel was seated on the sand at the foot of Wharf House, his back against its outer wall while he looked out across the harbour and at the people frolicking in the shallows—a peaceful summer idyll.

I won't stand for it anymore!

His father's voice came to him then, as a bolt from the blue.

It has to stop!

"What has to stop, Dad?" he wondered aloud. "What were you talking about?"

He remembered those two lines clearly, and had told the police team at the time—a team headed by a young Harry Pearce, who was now the local Detective Chief Superintendent.

There was nobody else around, son, Pearce had told him, with a tender smile for the bereaved. *How could you have heard anything from all the way inside the house? I'm sorry, Gabe, but it doesn't help for you to invent stories at a time like this.*

That's right, kid, listen to your Uncle Harry, Derek Tailor had intoned.

We all want to believe there was a reason for this, Gabe, Arthur told him, later on. *Sometimes, we come to the end of the road, and that was the way for your father. I'm sorry, lad, I really am.*

The mind plays tricks, Gabe, Tom Cutter had said. *It's a tragedy, that's what it is, but the sea must be respected.*

They were wrong.

There'd been no invention, no trick of a young boy's mind, and he knew that now beyond a shadow of a doubt. Those were the words his father had cried out, which had carried on the wind to his son's open window a couple of storeys above.

By Gabriel's reckoning, his father must have been standing very near to where he now sat, thirty years later, right next to the access door to the underground cellars of the house, a doorway often used by the family as a shortcut onto the beach.

Dad? Are you all right?

He remembered clambering out of bed and running downstairs, expecting to find his father passed out on the sofa or the floor, as usual. But he was not there, nor anywhere else in the house. The lights were on, and a half-drunk bottle of wine sat open on the dining table, but there was no trace of John Rowe. His younger self had pulled on a hoodie and taken the cellar stairs, his bare feet moving silently against the damp stone steps until he reached the lower storage area, where he wished he'd bothered to grab some flip-flops. The voices had gone, by then, but the door leading onto the beach stood ajar and there was a smell of something earthy on the air, something he couldn't place.

He didn't stop to wonder what it was, but headed out onto the beach which shone an iridescent white in the thin light of a crescent moon. He looked for his father, a lone figure stumbling over the sand or lying slumped on the beach with a bottle in hand.

There was nobody there.

Dad?

Dad!

Frightened, alone, he'd searched all around the harbour but found nothing. The darkness was all consuming, and it was not until first light that John Rowe was discovered by a local fisherman.

When the knock came at the door, Gabriel had been dressed and ready, his gangly, boyish frame held stiffly from a night spent in the big old house worrying and preparing himself for the worst.

Then, the worst came.

I'm sorry, Gabe, it's your father…

He was sorry, too, but not as sorry as his father's killer would be, before he was done.

───────

Somebody else was pounding at the front door by the time Gabriel made his way back up the cellar stairs and into the main part of the house.

"Sophie," he said, as his face broke into a smile. "And this must be the famous PC Turner."

The young constable began to smile in return, before remembering the reason for their visit.

"Mr Rowe, we'd like a few minutes of your time, please."

Gabriel frowned at the stilted formality, but told himself it was probably how she differentiated 'work' and 'home'. "Of course," he said, keeping the smile on his face. "Why don't you come into the living room?"

She couldn't stand to question him in the room where, only hours before, she'd lain with him, trusted him, poured her heart out to him, like a trusting fool.

She couldn't stand it.

"The kitchen would be better, if you don't mind."

Her voice was definitely frosty, and he wondered if it was for the benefit of her constable. Whatever the reason, he didn't care for it.

"This way," he said.

"Mr Rowe, we're here in connection with the murder of a man we believe to have been Dean Mostend," she said, without any further small talk. "We'd like to interview you under caution, back at the station."

Gabriel stared at her. "I have nothing to do with his death."

"Gabriel Rowe, you do not have to say anything, but it may harm your defence if you do not mention when questioned something you later rely on in court. Anything you do say may be given in evidence."

"You're *arresting* me, now?"

"No, I'm reciting the standard caution, for your own protection. Do you understand it, and would you like to exercise your right to legal representation?"

"I don't need any bloody representation!" he burst out, his eyes beseeching her to stop the nonsense.

Sophie told herself to remain strong, no matter what had passed between them.

"Am I to understand you're waiving your rights at this time?"

"I'll answer any of your questions," he said, in a cold voice. "All you ever have to do is ask."

"I'm glad you're willing to be cooperative," she said. "Perhaps you can start by telling us exactly what you were doing on Wednesday evening?"

Gabriel understood the mistake he had made, and heaved a sigh. "I know what this is about," he said. "I visited Dean's apartment building last week, and I forgot to mention it."

Sophie's expression did not alter, and he would later admire her for that.

"For what purpose did you visit Mr Mostend's home?"

"To make him an offer for his painting, as I've told you before."

Sophie's eyes flashed once, in anger. "You told me you were interested in purchasing *Moonlit Bay*, yes. However, when asked directly about when you'd last seen Mr Mostend, you told me you'd talked to him on wharf, last Wednesday morning. You neglected to mention that you'd paid him a further visit at his home the next day. PC Turner and I would very much like to know the reason why you omitted that information."

"For goodness' sake, it's nothing sinister," he said. "I wanted to know more about his inspiration for the painting, and why he chose to include the smuggling aspect."

He was particularly interested in that.

"Why did you feel the need to withhold this from the police, if there was nothing sinister?" Turner said, taking the words out of her mouth.

"I should have mentioned it," he agreed. "The fact is, Mostend wasn't at home, so I didn't think it was relevant. Besides, you weren't investigating him in connection to a murder, then; only in connection with the theft of his painting."

"That makes no difference," she snapped, although it probably did, and Turner opened his mouth to say as much, before closing it again in self-preservation.

Just then, her mobile phone began to buzz inside her pocket and, with an irritable sigh, she reached for it, intending to bin the call.

Irwin, the screen told her.

In a swift change of direction, she stepped out of the room and took the call from the forensics team.

"Thought you'd want to know," he said. "The DNA results on our John Doe have come in, and there's a match to a name on the system…in fact, there are a couple of matches."

A couple? she thought. *How was that possible?*

The forensics specialist sounded awkward all of a sudden. "I—ah—I thought it best to call you myself—"

"Well?" she prompted him. "Give me the good news."

Irwin cleared his throat.

"The body belongs to a man by the name of Michael Gallagher," he said, and waited for her to say something in response. When nothing was forthcoming, he carried on. "As you may already be aware, he was convicted of murder and served his time at Frankland Prison, in Durham. He was released a couple of months ago on compassionate grounds and, in fact, the pathologist confirms the presence of a very large tumour in the prefrontal cortex. If he hadn't wound up where he did, he would likely have died in a matter of weeks."

Still, Sophie said nothing as a siren continued to scream inside her head.

"The DNA was a fifty per cent match for another name on our database," he said quietly. "It was your name, Sergeant Keane."

All police officers submitted to having their DNA listed on the database, so they could be readily eliminated from an investigation on account of being part of the investigating team entering a crime scene. Usually, it helped them to isolate alien DNA samples, which they could focus on.

Occasionally, it helped to identify them as the living relatives of convicted killers.

"Thank you," she said, very softly.

"I—ah—I'll need to make my report soon," he said, and she was sorry for the position she'd put him in.

"Don't hold anything back," she reassured him. "Say exactly what needs to be said, and submit your report at your earliest convenience."

"Will you be—?"

"I'll be fine, thank you Pete," she said, and ended the call.

It seemed her time had run out, and so had Michael Gallagher's.

CHAPTER 24

"Did you know?"

Gabriel looked across to where Sophie stood in the doorway of his kitchen, and noted the loss of colour and glazed expression in her eyes that hadn't been there a few minutes before.

"Did I know *what*?" he asked, carefully.

PC Turner felt the charge in the room, and wondered what to do for the best.

"Perhaps we should pause the interview, for now?" he suggested.

But they didn't hear him, lost as they were in a battle of wills.

"Did you know that Dean Mostend was my father?" she said. "And that 'Dean Mostend' wasn't his real name, but an alias for Michael Gallagher?"

Turner's eyes widened, and he tried desperately to recall what the manual said about managing situations such as these, before remembering that there was no protocol for when a senior officer's estranged father—who happened to be a killer— turned up dead on a beach bearing the hallmarks of his own past crimes, having lived under an alias for at least a month before it.

It wasn't covered in the 'Troubleshooting' section, either.

"We should take some time—" he said.

"I asked you a question," she growled. "*Did you know*?"

"Of course I didn't know!" Gabriel almost shouted. "What the hell do you take me for?" His eyes burned a molten silvery-blue, fuelled by anger and, beneath it, hurt.

Sophie turned away, unsure of what to say or whom to trust. He seemed genuine, and there was no reason or connection she knew of between him and her late father. No reason at all for him to kill the man, but then, she hardly knew him and there were many layers to a person that took years to uncover. All she did know for certain was that Gabriel was in the area, both at the time of the theft of Dean Mo—of *Michael Gallagher's* painting, and within a likely timescale when he could have died. She wanted to believe his story about making an offer for the painting and chatting over the composition, but it just didn't wash. There was more to it than that, but she was too distraught to see the wood for the trees.

"I think we should all take a break," Turner tried again and, reluctantly, she nodded.

"I—yes. Yes."

She stumbled away, making for the front door, and Turner hurried to catch up with her but, before he could, Gabriel tapped him on the shoulder.

"Her mother's place," he murmured. "Take her to Jacqui's place, Scents of Cornwall, on Island Square. She needs her, and they'll need each other."

Turner, who happened to be a better judge of character than he was often given credit for, saw the substance of the man, and nodded his thanks.

"She has a cat, it might need feeding," Gabriel tagged on.

Turner smiled.

"Don't go anywhere," he said, and left Gabriel to wonder whether the message had been delivered from the police constable, or from Sophie's friend.

Jacqui spotted her daughter through the shop window, and one look was enough to have her hurrying out of the door and across the square to help Turner, who had taken Sophie's left arm in support.

"What is it?" she whispered. "What's happened, Sophie? Tell me!"

"He's dead," her daughter replied, in a toneless voice. "He's finally dead. He'd been here in St Ives the whole time, watching us."

"What?" Jacqui shook her head, not understanding.

"The body we recovered the other day has been identified," Turner explained. "It was Michael Gallagher. Sophie tells me he was her father."

Jacqui closed her eyes and allowed the feeling of relief to spread through her body, then turned to her daughter who was obviously struggling with the news.

"Come on," she said gently. "Thank you, Alex, I'll take it from here."

"I have to get back to work," Sophie said. "There's a lot to do, and I need to speak with the Super."

"That can wait," Jacqui said firmly, and Turner nodded his agreement.

"I'll handle anything that comes in until you're ready, boss."

Sophie gave a hollow laugh. "I won't be your boss for much longer, Alex."

"Don't say that," he implored.

"I lied to you," she said.

"You had your reasons, and they sound like pretty good ones, to me."

He turned to leave, paused, then did something that definitely wasn't in the Manual.

He gave his boss a quick, hard hug.

"Keep your chin up, Sarge," he said, before scurrying back towards the centre of town.

"He's a sweet boy," Jacqui remarked, which made her think of Gabriel. "Would you like me to call that lovely young man—?"

"No," Sophie said sharply, and her mother asked no more questions on that score.

"All right," she said. "Come on, sweetheart. I think it's time we let this all go, don't you?"

She put an arm around her daughter and led her to safety, as she'd done once, long ago.

———

"I never recognised him."

With the shop closed for the day, Jacqui had installed them both at her kitchen table which now held a smorgasbord of scones, flapjacks, crisps and anything else she could lay her hands on that was neither healthy nor nutritious.

There was a time and place for that, and this wasn't it.

Sophie cupped a steaming mug of tea in her hands, and let it warm her from the inside while she processed the news that Gallagher was dead, that the connection she'd tried to hide for a quarter of a century was now out in the open, and that she was likely to lose her position and her standing in the community she loved.

"What was that, love?"

Her mother looked up from where she was re-filling the kettle to make another pot of tea.

"I said, I never recognised him—my own father. Although, the word *father* sticks in my craw."

Jacqui nodded, and looked out of the kitchen window at a pair of pigeons cooing on the fence of her small, immaculately tended garden.

"It's been a very long time," she said. "You can't be expected to recognise him, after so long, and when he'd changed so much."

Sophie didn't bother to add that Gallagher's body had been so badly mangled, his face in particular, that it could have been an impossible task in any case.

"I might have told you this before, but there's never been a better time to repeat it," Jacqui said, turning to look at her child, who was now a woman—and a lovely one, at that. "For all his crimes, for all the heartbreak he caused me and so many other families, I can't ever regret having met Mick because, without him, there would never have been *you*."

Sophie's eyes filled with tears.

"I love you," her mother continued, and moved to wrap her arms around her daughter. "I'm sorry if I don't tell you often enough how proud I am of you, and everything you do for this town. I hope they remember that but, even if they don't, I certainly will, and so will all the individual people you've helped."

Sophie let the tears fall, and allowed herself to be rocked against her mother's breast, just this one time when she needed it the most.

"I love you, too," she whispered. "Thank you for trying to protect me from it all, and for all the sacrifices you made—even the ones I don't know about."

Jacqui thought of the late nights spent delivering catalogues while Sophie was with her childminder, or the times she'd been forced to miss school plays because she had to work. She'd done her very best and, when she looked at her daughter, at her kindness and fortitude, she knew it had been enough.

Blinking away tears, she kissed the top of her daughter's head, then cupped her face between her hands.

"Whatever comes next, we'll deal with it together," she said. "He's gone now, and we're free."

"So is his killer," Sophie said.

Jacqui nodded, and sank onto a chair beside her.

"There's a certain poetic justice to a killer being killed himself," she said. "I don't believe in taking an eye for an eye, but I understand why some people would. You said somebody carved a fish on his arm?"

Sophie nodded. "It's very similar to the one he carved onto the arm of his victim, back in Newcastle," she said. "I compared the crime scene images and it's uncanny. Whoever did it obviously wanted us to think Gallagher himself was the perpetrator, but why?"

Jacqui shook her head. "If it looks like a professional job, it might be payback for an old score," she said. "Someone who couldn't get to him while he was banged up?"

Sophie considered the options. "The painting must be important, somehow," she said. "I can't figure out how, but it's a key, I know it is."

Jacqui reached for a scone and took a healthy bite. "You know, we've been working on the assumption that Mick knew we were both here," she said.

"It's reasonable to assume he used his connections to find our whereabouts," Sophie agreed.

"Yes, but…what if we he *wasn't* here because of us?" she said. "What if Mick didn't have the foggiest clue we lived in St Ives, and he came for some other reason? I just wish I knew what the reason could be."

Sophie began to think her mother might be on to something.

"The only way to try and find out is to speak to his former cellmates," she said. "He spent fifteen years inside, and he must have told someone of his plans once he was set free."

Jacqui raised a maternal finger. "Don't even think about it," she said.

"I have to fly up there and speak to them," Sophie argued. "Pearce is probably going to kick me off the investigation, and probably tell me to take a long sabbatical until he figures out how to manage me out to avoid reputational damage to the Force. If I catch a flight this evening and arrange things with the prison staff before close of business today, I can be there in time for visiting hours tomorrow morning. He was a bad person, but bad people still deserve justice. That's how it works."

Jacqui gave her daughter's hand a squeeze. "Be careful," she said. "Somebody out there wasn't afraid to kill someone like Gallagher, so they won't be afraid to act again, if they have to."

Sophie gave a brief nod. "I had the same thought myself."

"Like mother, like daughter."

They both smiled.

CHAPTER 25

"You're not coming with me."

"I am, and there's nothing you can do about it. I booked tickets for the pair of us."

Sophie paused in the act of opening her car door, and faced him across the bonnet.

"Turner, so help me, I'll write you up for insubordination."

"With the greatest of respect, Sarge, you need a wingman."

"This isn't *Top Gun*. Besides, I've spoken to more convicts than you've had hot dinners. It'll be a walk in the park."

"Yeah, well, consider it part of my ongoing training."

Sophie checked the time, which was shortly before seven o'clock, swore softly, and then jerked her head towards the passenger door.

"Fine. Get in, because I don't have time to argue. But I'm telling you now, there'll be no *Ibiza Party Anthems* playing on the way to the airport."

"What about *Old Skool 90s Hits*?" he asked, as they strapped themselves inside her nippy little Fiat.

"That's more like it," she muttered. In times of crisis, there wasn't much that couldn't be cured by *The Spice Girls,* though she'd sooner cut out her own tongue than admit that to another living soul.

Once they'd braved the narrow, winding roads out of St Ives and had joined the dual carriageway that would take them east towards Newquay airport, she spoke again.

"I don't understand why you're here, Alex. I'm making a trip that flies in the face of every professional protocol, after revealing a problematic familial connection with our victim. By rights, I should withdraw from the investigation—which I fully intend to do, after this trip is complete. But you don't need to come along for this or take any risks. You have a great career ahead of you."

"It's what friends are for," he mumbled, and turned a deep shade of red that had her wondering whether he suffered from an underlying heart condition.

She looked across at the young man who'd come to be like a brother to her, and then kept her eyes firmly on the road ahead.

"In that case...thanks."

Turner smiled at the passing scenery, and then clicked 'play' so the interior of the car was filled with the dulcet tones of *Viva Forever*.

"One thing that occurs to me," she said, after a few seconds passed.

"What's that?"

"If it ever gets back to the station house that I know all the words to this song, the mere fact I'm the daughter of a convicted killer will pale into insignificance."

"Sarge, I think your 'hard woman' reputation was shot after the incident with *Cotton Eye Joe*."

"Can't argue with that. Now, turn up the damn volume, so my old lady ears don't have to strain so much."

Hours later, after an existential journey on what Sophie would have described as a glorified tin pot with wings, followed by a meaningful exchange with the bloke in charge of the hire car she'd ordered, they made it safely to their hotel, which was a bog-standard affair just outside Durham city centre and located as near to the prison as she could find.

It even had running water.

"No offence, Sarge, but if I die from carbon monoxide poisoning in my sleep, tell my mother I love her, okay?"

"There's that insubordination again," she said, but harboured similar thoughts herself. "It's just a place to put our heads down. Besides, it was all I could find at short notice."

"I thought it was Norman Bates behind the reception desk back there," he said, and gave a comedy shiver for effect. "Just promise me, if you find a stuffed animal inside your bed, you'll save yourself and drive straight back to the airport. I'll understand."

She couldn't help but laugh. "See you in the morning, Turner—I hope."

Shut inside the salubrious surroundings of her hotel room, she fell back onto the bed—which almost bounced her back onto her feet again—and gave in to emotional and physical exhaustion. They said that death was the great leveller, and 'they' weren't wrong; after all the years of the spectre of Michael Gallagher looming large over their heads, they'd built him into a kind of unstoppable being from which they'd never escape—it was anticlimactic to find that he bled, as they all did, and died, as they all would. The sight of his body on Porthgwidden beach was something that would stay with her for a very long time, possibly all her life, but she suspected that would still have been true had he been no relation to her at all. Some things you simply didn't forget.

It was hard to hate someone who'd been responsible for giving you life, and Sophie had spent years grappling with this basic truth. Though she owed him nothing, a part of her psyche felt that, if she could find the perpetrator responsible for killing him, she'd think of it as a final parting farewell and consider herself even. As her mother had said, perhaps there was a certain irony to the manner of his death, but it also went against everything she stood for, and continued to stand for.

There wasn't very much she could control in the big, wide world, least of all the free will of others, but she could live by her own principles, even when it might have been easier to close the book on Mick Gallagher and leave him to rot.

Later, after she'd sampled the aforementioned running water and treated herself to a lukewarm bath, Sophie crawled between the sheets and put her head down on the pillow. Of all the things that had happened that day, all the memories that could have swarmed her fertile mind, it was only one face she thought of as her eyelids drooped.

Gabriel.

She remembered the comforting feel of his arms around her and yearned for them—and for him.

CHAPTER 26

The next day

His Majesty's Prison Frankland was a grim edifice.

Little more than a squat, red-brick structure, it had been designed for function rather than form, which befitted a facility destined to house some of the most dangerous Category A criminals in the land. It was a stark counterpoint to the nearby cathedral at Durham, a UNESCO World Heritage Site famed for its dazzling architecture and prominent vantage point atop a hillside with far-reaching views over the county. The residents of Frankland's maximum-security wing could look forward to an uninspiring view of some ill-tended lawn or a concrete exercise yard, at best.

Sophie had spent a disturbed night remembering her childhood in the North East, her mind replaying the bittersweet memories of days spent on the beach eating ice creams from Minchella's or playing in the park at the end of the road with her childhood friend, Emily. She remembered sitting beside her father watching *Pinocchio*, and seeing her mother and father laughing together in the kitchen. However, these rosy snapshots were tempered by the knowledge that they didn't portray the full picture; if she really forced herself to remember, she would recall times her mother had argued with her father about being late home again, without ever telling her where he'd been. Mick Gallagher had never laid hands on his wife or child, choosing to save his violence for others, but life ran according to *his* plans and there was little room for debate. Now, as they made their way up to the main entrance of Frankland, she could scarcely imagine the same proud, indomitable man spending the majority of his adult life caged behind its walls.

Then again, she couldn't imagine him taking another person's life, but the truth was a matter of public record.

"You okay, boss?"

She'd almost forgotten Turner was there, walking quietly along the pathway beside her. "Just taking in the scenery."

Presently, they arrived at the security office, and went through the motions of signing themselves in. Security was a protracted process lasting almost thirty minutes, involving manual and digital checks, until finally they were given the 'all clear' and were buzzed through a series of security doors, at the end of which was a holding area where they were told to wait.

"Detective Sergeant Keane, Constable Turner?"

They stood up to greet the prison warden, a short, muscular man by the name of Brian Tunnock, who wouldn't have looked out of place among a line-up of inmates.

"Thank you for allowing us to visit at such short notice," Sophie said, taking his outstretched hand.

"Not at all," he replied. "Although, I feel I should warn you that Clive Robinson isn't one of our most talkative members of the community here. I hope your journey won't turn out to be a wasted one."

The only thing being wasted was time, Sophie thought, but there was nothing to be done about it. Things moved at their own pace, whether she liked it or not.

"Here we are," the warden said, as they approached a nondescript looking door. "Get yourselves settled in here, and I'll have Robinson brought along."

They thanked the warden again and took up a seat inside one of their individual meeting rooms which were reserved for inmates' appointments with legal counsel or police interrogation. It was almost a carbon copy of one of the rooms in the interview suite back home, having a single table in the centre of the room that was bolted to the floor for safety, four chairs—also bolted in place—and no natural lighting, just a series of strip lights that shone a grey-white light that wouldn't have looked out of place in the mortuary.

"Who is this guy, anyway?" Turner asked, setting a mobile recorder on the table alongside a notebook and his favourite pencil.

"Keep the pencil in your hand, for now," she said mildly. "Clive Robinson is around eighty but, in his heyday, he was known as the 'Gentleman Caller'. He sweet-talked his way into the homes of a lot of old women, whom he often attacked, sometimes killed or left for dead. He was a brutal sadist, and used whatever weaponry was to hand."

There was no time for Turner to reply to that before the outer door opened again to reveal an old man dressed in grey sweatpants and a sweater, his wrists hand-cuffed and flanked by two sharp-looking prison officers. He looked nothing like the kind of man who could possibly have committed the crimes he had, but that was part of his fatal charm—they never saw him coming.

They led him to one of the chairs opposite Sophie and Alex, and then secured his wrists to a smaller eye bolt on the edge of the table, which allowed a limited range of movement. Sophie wondered whether to request that they be loosened, but decided to keep the offer up her sleeve as a bargaining tool, in case he should prove difficult to crack. One of the officers left the room after that, while the other stationed himself on a stool in the corner, ready to step in if necessary.

"Thank you for meeting with us today, Mr Robinson," she said. "I'm Detective Sergeant Sophie Keane, of the Devon and Cornwall Police, and this is my partner, Constable Alex Turner."

"Only a sergeant?" Robinson tutted. "I'd have thought I warranted at least an inspector."

"You'll have to make do with me," she shot back. "Would you like a drink?"

"Whisky," he replied.

"The choice is tea, coffee or water."

"Pity. In that case, I'll have a mug of the watered-down sludge that passes for coffee in this place. Two sugars."

Turner rose without her needing to ask him, and dipped outside to head to the vending machine further down the corridor. In the minutes he was gone, she was fully appraised by the old man, whose myopic blue eyes helped themselves to every part of her he could see, and left her feeling violated.

"Pretty thing," he said. "Mick always said you would be."

Which answered at least one question, Sophie thought. Her father had known who she was, and had told Clive Robinson, too. How else would the old man know she was any relation of Gallagher's?

It stood to reason, then, that her father had also known she was living in St Ives, so his decision to travel there following his release from prison was no accident. Still, he'd spent nearly two months living in the town without approaching her or her mother. He'd gone about his business, painted his pictures and been a normal member of the community during that time.

Was his death simply a case of his past having caught up with him, as the marking on his body would suggest?

The door opened again, and Turner returned balancing four cups of coffee, one of which he offered to the prison officer, who was clearly surprised to have been included.

"Thanks, mate, appreciate that."

When she wasn't so focused on her task, Sophie would later congratulate her protégé on remembering the small things. Should they ever need to ask a favour from that officer, he would remember the small kindness shown to him and be more likely to help them in future.

"Did I miss anything?" Turner asked them.

"Oh, I think I just gave your boss here a little shock." Robinson chuckled to himself, and wrapped his long, bony fingers around one of the cups. "I don't think she realised we all know who she is around here, and have done for quite some time."

Sophie took a scalding sip of her own coffee, and made sure she was sitting well back from the table, out of reach of any 'accidental' spillages.

"It seems my father found out about my new identity," she acknowledged. "That isn't any great surprise to me, nor that he decided to tell you about it."

"We were friends for a long time," Robinson said, embellishing the truth a bit. After all, when the system throws two people together in a confined space, and both of them unafraid to kill, it makes sense to befriend one another rather than live with an enemy. "You're lookin' for him, I s'pose? I warn you, Mick always said he'd never let anybody take him alive."

Sophie realised he hadn't heard the news, not even on the prison grapevine.

"Michael Gallagher was found dead a few days ago," she said bluntly. "He was murdered."

That wiped the smile from his face.

"He was ill," he said. "Brain tumour, of all things."

"He was murdered," she said.

Robinson seemed genuinely shocked to hear it. "Back in the day, Mick had a few scores left unsettled, and there might've been one or two who would've brained him if they had the chance," he said, not bothering to mince his words. "But now? I can't think who'd want to waste their time. He was dying, anyhow."

"I'd like to find out who killed him," she said. "I was hoping you might be able to help us."

"Aye, that's right. You look out for your old dad," he said, and something turned in Sophie's stomach, for that wasn't how she'd describe her motivations. She was an officer of the law, and considered tracking down her father's killer to be a duty she would have discharged for anyone following their death, regardless of whether she happened to like them very much in life. However, if it helped to elicit information, she'd let Robinson believe she'd come as the prodigal daughter, eager to avenge her father's death.

"Mick wasn't half as bad as someone like me," Robinson remarked.

He said it casually, and, as an idle boast, it seemed ridiculous coming from a man of his advanced years. However, Sophie tried never to judge by appearances; a snake was still a snake, even when it was an old snake.

"What makes you say he wasn't as bad as you?"

"You have to understand something, sweetheart. Being inside here for so long can either break or make a man. Some of them go off their bleedin' rockers. Others find something to make themselves useful, take up reading, painting, drug-dealin'...all that. Mick decided to be creative, and used his hands. Nobody in here would've dared say anythin' about it, either."

"Did he have a rep in here?"

Robinson took a long drink, then set the cup down again. "He came in with a rep, he left with a rep. A few times he had to defend himself, so he did what he had to do. It cost him a month in solitary confinement every time, but they didn't come for him again. If you're thinking anybody in here would have gone for him, you're wrong. He didn't have any enemies in here; people respected him."

Sophie didn't want to think about prison fights or shivs between the ribs, nor about her father being a talented artist. It seemed like an insult to the dead, and to their families, for him to have been blessed with something so rare, while he had taken something even rarer from all of them— a human life.

"Did he talk to you about his plans, what he would do if he was ever released from prison?"

"Sure." Robinson polished off the last of his cup, then leaned back as far as he could while remaining tethered to the table. "But since you've already found him, it seems unnecessary for me to tell you that he planned to go to St Ives."

"Did he say what he wanted to do, when he arrived there?"

Robinson nodded. "He wanted to reconnect with you. He told me he'd sell some of his paintings, make a load of money, and be able to provide for you."

"I wouldn't have wanted it," she muttered.

"It isn't about what you want," Robinson pointed out. "You asked me what he wanted. That was it."

She nodded. "You've been very cooperative," she said. "Why?

"Because Mick Gallagher was the closest thing I ever had to a friend in here," he replied.

CHAPTER 27

Gabriel slept in far later than usual, and awoke with a splitting headache.

"Bugger," he muttered, and went in search of some tablets to relieve the pain. While he waited for them to do their work, he showered and dressed, and then made his way downstairs in search of water, believing his headache to have been caused by dehydration as temperatures continued to rise. He should have been used to the climate, by now, but it seemed even native Cornishmen could feel the after-effects of too much sun.

Entering the kitchen, he was met with a stale smell of alcohol, which immediately dredged up memories of the mornings he used to wake up for school to find no bread or cereal in the cupboard, but a lingering scent of booze and a pile of empty bottles discarded in the bin.

"Must be another sensory memory," he told himself, and shook his head as if to clear away the smell. "It isn't real."

But then, his eye caught on the recycling bin, which had been left open since he'd last used it to dispose of a carboard box. Gabriel looked at it for a long moment, then walked slowly across the room, hand raised to close it again.

But his hand froze as soon as he caught sight of the contents.

Instead of the usual flattened cereal boxes or delivery parcels and old letters, the recycling bin was full to the brim with empty wine and beer bottles.

Gabriel took an involuntary step backward, feeling the blood rush in his ears.

Be a good lad, and put those outside for me, eh, Gabe?

His father's voice came to him again, as clear as a bell.

"It's not real," he repeated, and closed his eyes for a few seconds, using the meditation techniques he'd been taught.

But when he opened his eyes again, the bottles were still there.

He backed out of the kitchen towards the living room, where he found the sofa cushions in disarray, as if somebody had fallen onto the floor. On the coffee table, a glass had smashed against its wooden top and the remains of some red wine had stained the oak and the floor beneath.

"What's happening here?" he whispered.

He hurried back into the kitchen and made a grab for the recycling bin, eager to dispose of its contents. His head continued to pound and he saw dark spots dancing in front of his eyes. Abandoning the bottles, he leaned back against the countertop and then sank onto the tiled floor, clutching his head in his hands.

What was happening?

Was he going mad?

He had no memory of drinking anything the previous night, let alone several bottles to himself. Even when Sophie had been with him the night before, they'd chosen tea over alcohol.

He tried to retrace his steps of the previous day, but found the exercise far more difficult than it should have been. After Sophie had thrown her accusations in his face, and Turner had taken her away, rather than harbouring a sense of anger, he'd worried about her for the rest of the day. He'd tried to distract himself with work, which had killed a couple of hours, then he'd gone for a walk on the beach where he'd devoted himself to the task of building an enormous sandcastle, which was another focused task that distracted him from thoughts of angry brunette law enforcement officers for another couple of hours. After handing over the upkeep of the castle to a young boy by the name of Jamie, who was out walking with a man he introduced as Nick, his 'New Daddy', and whom he seemed to remember meeting at the gallery opening, Gabriel had bidden them both farewell and returned to Wharf House via the fish 'n' chip shop, where he'd ordered the house special: whale and chips.

He'd eaten his food on the way home and let himself back into the house, only to be disturbed by a knock on the door a short while later. It had been Jenna Pearce bearing a wicker 'welcome basket' full of shortbread biscuits, tea and homemade banana bread, which he was happy to accept but not in return for the rest of his afternoon, which was something she clearly hoped for.

Thanking her for the kind thought, he'd sent her packing as politely as he could, before a second interruption had come from the postman delivering a package containing an advance copy of a book due to be published soon from a debut author hoping for a kind quote to help it fly.

He'd read a few pages, eaten a slice of banana bread, drank a cup of tea, and begun to feel tired. He and Sophie had been up late the previous evening, so he'd put it down to a mild case of sleep deprivation, and had taken himself upstairs for an early night.

That was all he remembered.

And yet, the empty bottles remained, taunting him, whispering to him from the past and telling him he was just like his father.

And he'd end up just like him, too.

———

Later, when they'd retraced their steps through endless checkpoints and stepped out into the fresh air once again, Sophie looked up at the steel-grey sky, drew several deep breaths of air into her lungs and then turned to her constable.

"Thanks for sitting in on that," she said.

"No problem. Did you get what you were hoping for?"

She thought of her father's oil paintings adorning the walls of the communal areas, and of Robinson's claim that he'd changed beyond all recognition, casting aside his past to forge ahead as a new man, even within the maximum-security confines of Frankland Prison.

"If prison went some way to rehabilitating him, that would be a first," she said. "But at least I know more about him than I did before. For instance, Robinson confirmed why Gallagher was in St Ives, so we don't have to speculate any more about his reasons."

She didn't comment on how it made her feel to know he'd come back because of her, and she was grateful he hadn't ever made the final step to make contact directly and tell her who he was. Some things, and some relationships, were better left in the past.

"As for being any closer to understanding who might've wanted to kill him, we're still in the dark. I had a word with the local police the other day and they said they haven't heard any rumblings to do with Mick Gallagher for more than twenty years. He was old news on the gangland scene, forgotten and left to rot once he was put away. Perhaps that might've been different if he'd chosen to continue his exploits on the inside, but the warden confirmed to us that he was a model prisoner during the past ten years, in particular."

They walked back to the hire car, eager to leave Frankland behind them but as she reached for the door handle Sophie turned back to look one last time.

"His life could have turned out so differently," she said. "My mum told me that Michael came from a difficult childhood, where he saw a lot of things he shouldn't, and dealt with more trauma than he should have. I think she told me that so I'd have some kind of reason or excuse as to why he behaved the way he did. But in our line of work, we see people in hardship every day. They aren't all millionaire property owners with penthouses overlooking the beach; they're real people working hard to keep going, and that's the human condition. Some of them suffer childhood trauma, just as Michael did, but they don't decide to embark on a life of crime. They might have less money than someone dealing drugs to kids, but they have more self-respect and enough to get by."

She sighed and turned away again.

"The truth is, there's always some excuse," she said. "We can all find a reason to justify ourselves, if we really want to, but life is challenging for everyone. That's the human condition. It doesn't make other people expendable."

She realised it was time to stop making excuses for herself, too. Time to stop using her father as an excuse not to live her life and learn to trust people again, and time to stop lashing out at the people who tried to help her.

Her mother. Alex. Luke and Gabi, Nick and Kate, Gabriel...

Gabriel.

In the small hours of the morning, when she'd given up on the prospect of sleep, she'd logged onto her secure work system and completed a 'deep dive' on Gabriel Rowe, searching for any possible connection to Michael Gallagher that could justify her misplaced accusation that he'd been in league with her father, or had known of his identity all along, for some underhand reason connected to the man's death. Predictably, she'd found nothing but evidence of an upstanding citizen who paid his taxes on time and had no criminal record whatsoever. Instead, public records told her of a man who gave a sizable percentage of his personal income to children's hospitals who specialised in treating the most difficult and complex cases, and the ongoing donations had now accumulated in the millions.

That didn't mean Gabriel wasn't a killer, of course, but she had to admit that large-scale philanthropy, general chivalry and a clean police record wasn't a killer's usual MO.

"Are we going home, then?"

Turner's voice interrupted her reverie, and she started up the engine.

"Yeah," she said. "It's time to face the music."

CHAPTER 28

Duty called again, this time quite literally, soon after Sophie and Alex touched down at Newquay airport, shortly after three o'clock. Apparently, a briefing had been arranged in her absence at the constabulary's Bodmin Headquarters, and she was required to attend.

Before the crown courts moved to Truro, Bodmin had been the county town of Cornwall, being one of the oldest major settlements and indeed the only one to have been recorded in the Domesday Book. Nowadays, it was a convenient administrative stronghold in the centre of the county, and the police had chosen to site their regional headquarters there for convenience more than historic interest.

The building was at least a newly-built structure with plenty of space and working toilets, which was more than they could regularly boast back at the station in St Ives. However, whatever it might have had in the way of unstained carpets and clean changing rooms, the building lacked in terms of basic kerb appeal. Thus, when Sophie and Alex drew into the staff car park, they encountered a strong feeling of déjà vu, since its boxy lines bore more than a passing similarity to Frankland Prison.

"Need a coffee?" Turner asked, as they stepped inside the foyer.

Sophie was already making a beeline towards the vending machine. "What's that?"

"Never mind."

Armed with provisions, they made their way through the security gates and upstairs to the executive level, feeling like dead men walking.

———

"DS Keane, PC Turner, thank you for joining us. Please, take a seat."

Despite their being exactly on time for the briefing, it was immediately clear to Sophie that those already present had convened at an earlier time, no doubt to discuss the revelations about her parentage and to come to a decision about what they would do about it. Whilst she was on tenterhooks to know how the brass decided to play with her future, she still had work to do and would do it to the best of her ability until they told her not to.

DCS Pearce was chair of the briefing, and opened the conversation.

"DS Keane, there are a few matters to discuss but, to begin with, I think we'd all appreciate an update regarding the status of the St Ives murder investigation, if you wouldn't mind. I should tell you, we've already had sight of the forensic examiner's report," he added, so there could be no misunderstandings.

She could never fault Harry Pearce for being anything other than scrupulously polite.

"Certainly, sir," she said, and licked dry lips. "As you know, the body we discovered on

Friday morning was mutilated to such a degree that it was impossible to make any sight-based identification. Manual checks of Missing Persons didn't elicit any real possibilities, so we were relying heavily on DNA-based ID matching with a name already on the system. In the meantime, we began to think our unidentified body belonged to a local artist, Dean Mostend, whose painting was stolen from the new gallery in St Ives a couple of days before and which I'll come on to, sir."

"Are you treating the cases as linked?"

"I believe we have to," she replied.

"All right," Pearce said. "Carry on—what put you on to Dean Mostend?"

"The trousers, sir," she replied. "They were recovered near where the body was found, and enquiries with local vendors confirmed they were purchased only recently, around a month ago, at one of the shops in St Ives."

She went on to explain their questioning of Alissa, and subsequent application for a search warrant.

"We recovered a jacket from the apartment which was also detailed on the shop's receipt, and it was an exact match. Forensics have now swept the full apartment leased to Dean Mostend, and I understand they're due to submit a report on their findings any day now."

"Already done," Pearce said, blindsiding her. "Given the unusual circumstances, I felt an express service was in order."

To stay ahead of any revelations, she realised.

"Thank you," she said, and was careful to keep any sarcasm from her tone. "May I ask what the forensics report summary said? Having just landed and come straight from the airport, neither PC Turner nor myself have had any opportunity to read it ourselves."

Pearce produced a copy for them both, and Sophie took one, scanning the contents with a meticulous eye.

"Irwin is of the opinion a large amount of human blood was lost in the centre of the living space at Mostend's flat," Pearce said. "He thinks it most likely a rug was down, and then used to help to dispose of the body later on. Meanwhile, an extensive clean-up operation took place which, sadly, removed much of the blood spatter but not that which remained deep in the grouting. There, his team were able to extract minute DNA samples and run a check against names. I believe you're aware of the rest, DS Keane."

The moment had come, she realised.

Her stomach rolled, but she was no coward and faced the room without shame.

"Yes, I am," she said. "I was alerted to the fact a DNA match had been found for our DB, belonging to a 'Michael Gallagher', whom some of you might remember from more than twenty years ago, when he was brought up on a murder charge, and convicted as one of the senior members of a gang based out of the North East."

Beneath the conference table, she clasped her hands together to prevent them from shaking.

"What you probably won't know is that Gallagher was my father. Following his arrest, when I was four, my mother and I joined the Witness Protection Scheme and moved down here to St Ives, where I've lived ever since. We had no contact with him, and assumed different names as part of the Scheme. When the body was first discovered, it bore a marking in the shape of a fish. This was a close replica of a fish carved into the body of one of my father's victims, which was reported in the press at the time and kept on police file. When I saw that marking, my first instinct was to wonder whether my father had escaped or been released from prison, and had been responsible for killing that unidentified person."

Her voice shook, ever so slightly, and she took a swig of coffee to steady it.

"Following up on this suspicion, I rang Frankland Prison to ascertain my father's whereabouts, and was informed he'd been released two months prior, on compassionate grounds. His whereabouts were unknown. At that time, I considered him my prime suspect, but had no proof whatsoever. I also want to say that I had no knowledge that he was living under an alias, Dean Mostend, and had been living in St Ives throughout that time. I did not recognise him when we assessed the cadaver, and I did not recognise him on the few occasions when I saw Dean Mostend painting around the town. I had no occasion to speak with him, ever. PC Turner and I travelled to Frankland yesterday to speak with Gallagher's former cellmate, who affirmed that, to the best of his knowledge, there was nobody remaining in the gangland world who was seeking him out, as the carving of the fish on his upper arm would suggest."

She paused to catch her breath, and DCS Pearce exchanged a glance with his colleagues before leaning his elbows on the table and clasping his hands together in a manner she associated with someone preparing to impart some difficult news.

"Thank you for that summary, DS Keane," he said. "I've listened carefully, and must say there a couple of red flags that stand out, so I wonder if you're able to offer an explanation."

Here it comes, she thought.

"Firstly, when you saw that the body had been defaced with the image of a fish, and you suspected this to be the work of Michael Gallagher, your father, why did you not make the department aware of your suspicion at the earliest opportunity?"

At this, Turner could remain silent no longer.

"With respect, DCS Pearce, I remember very clearly that DS Keane told me she recognised the carving as being similar to the handiwork of the killer Michael Gallagher. Therefore, she did make her immediate team aware of the connection and alerted me to the possibility of it being a genuine lead to follow up. It was immaterial to mention that he was her father, and I believe she was trying to keep both realms separate, in the best traditions of professionalism, sir."

Sophie listened to his small, eloquent speech and thought that, one day, Alex Turner would be an ever greater man than he was now.

And he was already pretty great.

"That's all well and good, Turner, but there was a duty to disclose the potential of a familial connection."

"Sir—"

"Alex," she murmured, and reached across to put a gentle hand on his arm, to indicate he'd already done more than she could ever have expected of him. "Thank you, but I'll take it from here."

She turned back to the superintendent and his cronies.

"I agree, sir, I should have made the department aware of the connection sooner, but I suppose I thought the matter could be eliminated quickly once the DNA results came in, and we'd be able to track down the victim's known associates. I hoped it would not be relevant, sir."

"That your father was a notorious killer?" one of them scoffed, and a few others chuckled too.

She told herself not to crumble, not to give any of them the satisfaction of breaking down.

"Sir, this job, the people of Cornwall...they mean the world to me. There's a killer still at large, and there's every possibility they could strike again unless we get to the bottom of why Michael Gallagher was killed, and why they wanted to stage his murder to look as though he had, in fact, been the perpetrator. I think that's where the missing painting becomes relevant—"

"Detective Sergeant Keane," Pearce overrode her with ease. "Your failure to withdraw from an active case on account of there being an obvious conflict is worthy of disciplinary action. Quite apart from this personal matter, I must also say that neither the murder investigation nor the investigation into the theft of Mostend's—or rather, Gallagher's—painting has progressed very far. There are no witnesses to the painting having been taken, no further leads as to its whereabouts. As for the investigation into your father's murder, it seems whoever killed him has been able to do away with an old man like a professional, removing all traces to impede progress, apparently without an obvious motive. Your father was no ordinary person, so if his killer *was* aware of Gallagher's reputation, we must congratulate them on being brave, at the very least."

There were a few more witters around the room.

"Despite these failures, and following some discussion with my peers, we have decided to exercise compassion in light of your recent bereavement and suggest that, rather than be brought up on disciplinary charges, we acknowledge your long service, your passion and commitment to the job prior to this, and the extreme stress you must have been under when managing this particular joint investigation. For these reasons, we've decided to recall you from the investigation, Sergeant, and suggest that you take a period of compassionate leave."

Sophie had known it was coming, long before the words were spoken aloud. A part of her had been waiting for the moment when she'd be found out, and banished, for many years. But when she finally heard the message, it came as a punch to the belly.

"Of course," she said, in a voice heavy with tears. "I remain at the department's disposal, should you ever need me."

CHAPTER 29

Sophie found Gabriel sitting on an old bench beside St Ives Head, which was a historic lookout point with a coastal watch tower situated at the pinnacle of the island peninsula, with views across most of the bay and far beyond. Having spent what was left of the afternoon searching the beaches, the harbour, the shops and anywhere else she could think of to find him, it gave her heart a little stutter to finally stumble across him in one of the last places she had left to search.

"Can I join you?" she asked.

He turned in reflex, and she felt the force of eyes that were the same colour as the sea beyond. In that moment, she wished she had some of her father's talent for painting, for she'd have liked to capture him sitting there, his face in profile with the sun setting at his back.

"Have you come to arrest me?"

She shook her head, and remained standing where she was, with the sea wind blowing across her face. "I came to apologise," she said. "I should never have jumped to so many conclusions. I was upset and confused, but there was no call to behave the way I did. I'm sorry, Gabriel."

In his experience, remarkably few people in life could muster the courage to apologise, but he wasn't surprised to find Sophie was one of them.

He held out a hand for her to join him on the bench and, when their fingers linked, the problems of the day seemed so much more manageable than before.

"I'm sorry too," he told her, and turned to meet her eyes once more, so she could be sure he was sincere. "I should never have withheld the fact I'd been up to Dean's apartment, or caused you to doubt my word. It won't ever happen again."

She nodded. "Why did you?"

He looked away, but continued to hold her hand, never wanting to let it go. "This was one of my dad's favourite spots," he said softly. "I like to come here to work through a problem in my mind, because it's where we used to come and talk about difficult maths homework, or to discuss politics or philosophy. It's where he'd tell me the next instalment in the story he'd made up, or chat about old Cornish myths and legends. Sometimes, he'd talk about my mother, but those days were usually bad days that'd end with him passed out drunk."

She said nothing, only listened to him, loving the sound of his voice and the feel of his skin against hers.

"I didn't tell you about going to visit Dean Mostend, because I didn't want anybody else to know," he said. "You see, my father was murdered, Sophie, and I came here to find out who was responsible. I thought Dean might be able to tell me something useful."

"Because he was Michael Gallagher, and had criminal connections?" she queried.

"No, I told you, I had no idea that was his real identity. I wanted to talk to him because of his painting. I'd seen him working on it, then I caught sight of the finished piece in Luke's catalogue. The bigger part of the composition is the harbour at night, with starry skies and moonlit houses, but there's a small element to it that was of great interest to me. Dean had painted a scene showing a number of large barrels being unloaded beneath the arches of Smeaton's Pier, which is very close to the external access to Wharf House. I wanted to know if that was the stuff of his imagination, or whether he'd witnessed that himself."

"What if he had?" she said. "People must unload all sorts of things."

He shook his head. "Not in the dead of night, in stormy weather, and not in that quantity," he said. "Did you know, in the old days, it was common practice for smugglers to hide their haul from the customs and excise men by submerging barrels under the water and tying them to a weighted line, so they couldn't be seen beneath the surface. That meant the smugglers could retrieve the barrels at a later date, when it was safe to do so."

Sophie thought of the painting, and their struggle to understand its significance. Perhaps Gabriel had answered that question for them.

"I thought your father fell, Gabriel?"

"That's what the coroner concluded, following reports and witness statements submitted by my father's closest friends, one of whom is now your esteemed Superintendent. Between them, Harry Pearce, Tom Cutter, Derek Tailor and Arthur Trenthorn stifled any prospect of a murder investigation."

"You believe one of them is responsible, don't you?"

"Or all of them," he said. "All I know is that, in the intervening time, every one of them has prospered, and not in a small way, either. Trenthorn has his restaurant empire, which must have cost—and continues to cost—a pretty penny,

I'll bet. Tailor has his property business, and has done very well from it. Pearce has risen in stature, but, even so, I can't figure out how a public servant, even a senior one, can afford three luxury cars, a fat Rolex and a million-pound property in Carbis Bay."

He had a point, although she'd always assumed Pearce must be in a shedload of debt to sustain that kind of lifestyle.

"What about Cutter?" she asked.

He paused to allow a small walking party to pass by before answering.

"I can't figure that one out," he admitted. "If he's involved, I can't see where he's putting the money."

"I wish you'd told me this sooner."

"I have no evidence," he said. "Only my memories, common sense, and what my heart knows to be true."

She'd often worked from less than that.

"I've been put on sabbatical," she said. "I'm off the Gallagher case, and everything else, for at least three months."

He didn't waste words on empty platitudes, but lifted an arm and brought it around her shoulders to hold her close.

"Does this mean you're available to work freelance on a private murder investigation?"

She smiled against his chest. "What kind of payment terms are you offering?"

"What kind of terms would you accept?"

She listened to his heartbeat, and thought about living and learning to trust again. She had to start sometime, and there was only one person with whom she wanted to try. That was a truth that her heart knew.

"How about an upgrade from the guest room to the master bedroom?"

He looked down at her, and the light burnished his hair a gleaming blue-black against the sky.

"A tad onerous, but I think I can agree to that."

She opened her mouth to tell him what a *really* onerous term would look like, but the words never left her lips, which were instead captured by the warmth of his mouth beneath the setting sun.

CHAPTER 30

"She's off the case."

The men gathered in their usual meeting place and raised a friendly hand to those they recognised passing by, looking like nothing more than two lifelong friends chewing the fat on a summer's evening.

"That doesn't mean she'll stop digging," the other said. "She isn't the type to let things go."

They looked across the water, to where Wharf House was bathed in light, its windows blinking like eyes across the harbour.

"Neither is he."

"With a little push in the right direction, Gabriel could be persuaded to leave the past behind. He's vulnerable to his father's memory, and we can use that. The process has already begun. A few more pushes and he'll leave, one way or another."

"What if he doesn't do it himself?"

"Then we'll have to give him another push, won't we? The point isn't how we get rid of him, it's what people will believe. Once they hear about his morbid obsession with his father's death and the worrying drink habit he's developing, they'll think 'like father, like son' and chalk it up to another tragic end. Wharf House will come under new ownership, and we can start storing the barrels in the cellar again, like the good old days."

"What if he tells Sophie about it?"

"Tell her what? That he found a stack of empty bottles and the evidence of a hard night's drinking, but he *swears* it wasn't him, it was the Ghost of Wharf House? Sophie Keane has never been one to lose her wits over a man, and she's not about to start now, even if he has a pretty face."

"If she does, though—"

"There have been certain other developments regarding our dear sergeant," his friend said. "Things that could affect our operation."

"How so? She isn't in charge of the investigation anymore."

"It isn't that—it's Mostend, or should I say Gallagher? He was her father."

The other man nearly choked on his tutti-frutti ice cream.

"He was *what*?"

"It came as a surprise to everyone, even the lady herself, I understand."

They thought about the impact, and what it could mean for them both.

"When's the next drop?"

"Tomorrow night. We have to move the last batch before we pick up the new ones—there's another storm forecast."

They both looked out across the harbour towards the sea, and a point in the water where fifteen plastic drums filled with crystal methamphetamine and heroin were weighted down, out of sight beneath the waves.

"Gabriel wanted a meeting to discuss his dear old dad," the taller man said. "You know what I always say—there's no time like the present."

"What about the painting?"

"It's long gone. There's no way they'll ever find it amongst a mountain of rubbish and, even if they did, the coordinates Gallagher wrote on the back will be irrelevant once we move the barrels this evening. Even if somebody went out there to look, they'd find nothing but a few fish and a lot of water. Gabriel, on the other hand, is a problem we need to deal with swiftly."

"It's still a pity."

"It isn't personal, it's business. That motto has served us well all these years, hasn't it?"

His friend nodded.

"So, we're agreed?"

They toasted their ice cream cones.

"I need to tell you something."

Sophie, clad only in the suit given to her by Mother Nature, looked across to where Gabriel lay beside her, similarly naked and still recovering from his exertions, which had been impressively energetic.

"What?" she asked. "Don't tell me you're married."

He smiled, and looked across at her. "Not yet," he said, with a smile. "I was going to tell you about an incident this morning. I honestly don't know if I'm losing my marbles."

She thought he was joking, and was about to say as much, before she caught the serious expression marring his handsome face.

"When I woke up this morning I had a migraine, which is something that hardly ever happens. At first, I put it down to stressing about the object of my affection thinking I was a criminal of some kind—"

She groaned and covered her face.

"—but then, I came downstairs to find a stack of empty wine bottles in my recycling bin and on the bench in the kitchen. There was a broken wine glass in the living room and the place was in disarray."

"If you're trying to tell me you drowned your sorrows after our little brouhaha…"

"That's just it," he said. "I didn't touch a drop, never mind several bottles' worth. I don't know where any of it came from."

She turned onto her side and propped her head on her hand, to look at him. He told himself to remain focused on the matters in hand, and not the matters that would be in his hand in five to ten minutes' time, if he had his way.

"The thing is, everything looked so much like how things were when my dad was alive," he muttered. "I have the occasional auditory memory, which I've told you about, and it brought on plenty more. I couldn't remember the night before, not even getting into bed, so I'm worried I did drink all that junk, after all, and blacked out just like he used to do. It's history repeating itself—"

She studied his face, and saw none of the usual signs of alcohol or substance abuse.

"Wait a minute—you say you don't remember the evening? What's the last thing you remember?"

He told her, and the running order of his day up until then.

"Wait here—I'll be back in fifteen minutes, I'm just going to grab something from the back of my car."

He watched with open admiration as she leapt from the bed and began to tug on her clothing, hopping from one leg to the other. She made for the door then thought better of it and rushed back to plant a kiss on his lips.

"Fifteen minutes," she whispered.

Sure enough, Gabriel had barely had time to make himself a cup of tea before she'd returned, letting herself back into the house using the latch key and holding a small plastic sachet and a rubber tourniquet in her hand.

"Portable blood testing," she said, only slightly out of breath from her jog to Porthminster and back. "We keep some of these on hand to administer a test when we think someone could have been the victim of deliberate drugging, particularly date-rape drugs. I can call in a favour and have the sample tested. That would give us a definitive answer about whether or not you had any alcohol yesterday, as well as anything more sinister, if you're happy to submit to it."

In answer, he held out a bare arm.

"Go ahead—I'm not squeamish," were his last words.

———

"That's never happened before, I promise."

Sophie raised a single eyebrow, and offered him another custard cream, which she'd found in a biscuit tin in the kitchen.

"That's what all the manly men say, after they've fainted at the sight of their own blood being taken."

He laughed, and popped another biscuit in his mouth.

"Did you get what you needed?"

"In more ways than one," she said, to make him laugh again. "As for the sample, I'll send it off first thing in the morning and we'll see what we see. But, Gabriel, listen to me. Nothing about this feels like the Gabriel I know. Everything that I've seen from our time together tells me you're a man with enormous amounts of self-discipline...just look at how patient you've been with me."

He smiled, and sat up on the sofa so that he could pull her down onto his lap.

"What if I'm a secret binge drinker?" he said. "I was frightened of myself, when I found those bottles this morning, Sophie. I need to be honest about that."

She nodded. "I understand, and, if you have a problem that you're not aware of, there are people and organisations who can help. I'll help you too. But consider another angle to this, Gabriel—what if it was a nasty scare tactic?"

His brows drew together. "From whom?"

"The people you're looking for," she said. "You might have touched a nerve somewhere, or made them nervous. Perhaps they're trying to scare you off the scent, or have you believe you should leave again and never come back."

"They're out of luck," he said, and held her tightly in his arms. "I've found an even better reason to stay."

"Better than filial revenge?"

"Much better."

She was quiet for a minute, and all humour was gone from her voice when she spoke again.

"I think they must be the same person, or people, responsible for killing my father," she said. "It's all connected. You believe your father found out about their smuggling operation and wanted to put a stop to it, but they killed him before he had the chance to tell anyone what he knew. Years later, my father came along and found out about it somehow, perhaps purely by chance, as he was out painting one evening. When I spoke to his old cellmate, he told me Gallagher wanted to sell his paintings for a packet and give the money to me, as some kind of reparation. Luke tells me that the painting, while of a very good standard, would never have fetched more than a few thousand pounds because the artist known as Dean Mostend was entirely unknown, so there would have been a ceiling."

"So you think Gallagher hoped he'd be getting an inflated price from, let's say, a private buyer? Someone who realised what the painting really showed, and didn't want anyone else to see?"

She nodded. "I think they probably wanted to make a deal, but according to Luke again, Mostend was adamant the painting should go to the highest bidder in open competition. That wouldn't have pleased them very much, so they resorted to more drastic measures and killed him, instead, then stole the painting before it could be shown and disposed of it so that nobody would ever see his depiction of smugglers unloading the barrels late at night."

"But there's an image of the painting in the catalogue," Gabriel pointed out. "There must be something else about the canvas, not just the image on the front of it, that they needed to destroy."

Sophie agreed. "I was waiting to hear from the waste management company in St Austell," she said, with some frustration. "I had to surrender my work phone, so I won't know the outcome."

"Would Turner consider acting as a line of communication?" Gabriel asked.

"I couldn't ask him to go against the rules," she said. "Anyway, I taught him not to, and he has far too much respect for my principles to—"

Just then, her personal phone began to ring, and Gabriel was amused to note the ring tone was none other than the theme tune from *Murder, She Wrote*.

"We need to talk about that, later," he said, before she made a grab for it.

"Keane? I mean…Sophie?"

"It's me—Alex." Turner kept his voice low but, judging from the sound of heavy machinery in the background, there was no need. "Look,

I know I'm not supposed to be discussing any work-related stuff with you at the moment, but—"

"You're going to break the rules?"

"I was thinking about it."

"After I told you repeatedly not to?"

"Yep."

"I always knew you were insubordinate. C'mon, gimme the dirt."

Turner switched the phone to his other hand and looked over his shoulder to be sure.

"We found the painting," he said. "I'm at the waste management site now. It's pretty messed up, but there was something written on the back of the canvas. It's just two six-figure numbers, boss. I don't know what they mean, but it can't be a mobile phone number, can it?"

"Coordinates," Gabriel said simply, having overheard that snippet of the conversation. "They could be coordinates."

She made a note of the numbers Turner read out to her.

"Do you think it's helpful?" he asked.

Gabriel held up an image on the screen of his smartphone, which showed the location of those coordinates as being a spot half a mile out of the harbour, hidden in plain sight beneath the waterline.

"Alex, I think you might have just saved the day," she said, giving Gabriel a 'thumbs-up' motion. "We have a line on who we think could be behind everything, and I think you might have just stumbled across the location of their most prized possession. Now, all we have to do is catch them with their hands in the proverbial cookie jar."

"I could speak to Pearce," Turner offered.

"That's the last thing you should do," Sophie said, and went on to explain why. "This is the most important lesson I could ever teach you, Alex. It's to remember that we are public servants, and are never open to bribery—"

"What about last week, when you bribed me with a packet of Rolos in exchange for doing that talk over at the secondary school?"

"That was different, and I'll thank you not to interrupt when I'm laying some knowledge on your rookie brain."

"What do you need?"

"I need you to call in the Ghost Squad, and tell them it's Priority A."

"But Sarge, the Ghost Squad investigate bent coppers."

"I know," she said quietly. "Call them, just the same."

CHAPTER 31

"Another gin 'n' tonic."

The bartender at The Sloop made a show of shaking his head, but poured Gabriel another glass of the clear spirit with a splash of tonic, which he set beside the other drinks on the tray he'd prepared for the group seated at their usual table.

"Take it easy, now," he said, before sliding the tray across the bar.

Gabriel nodded, and with slow, deliberate footsteps, made his way back across the room.

"Here we are!" he declared, in a voice that was a little too loud for comfort. "This'll keep our cockles warm, won't it?"

Arthur, Derek, Harry and Tom each grinned at him, and raised their own glasses in salute.

"That's the spirit, lad," Arthur said, exchanging a glance with the others. "Sometimes, we all need to let loose amongst friends."

"It's what your father would have wanted—to see us all here, together," Harry added, clinking his glass with Gabriel's. "Bottoms up."

"To you, Dad," he said, and gulped several fingers of gin and tonic, as if it was water. "I hear him sometimes, y'know?"

"How d'you mean?" Tom took a sip of his beer, and watched the younger man closely over the rim.

"I mean…" Gabriel ran a hand over his face, as if to clear his vision. "I mean, I—I hear him, as if he's in the same room. He speaks to me."

The others looked amongst themselves, and, when Derek spoke, it was loud enough for the neighbouring table to overhear.

"Let me get this straight: you're saying you hear John's voice, even though he's been dead for nearly thirty years?"

Gabriel nodded miserably. "I know, it sounds crazy," he mumbled. "That's why I wanted to talk to you all. I thought…maybe, if I get some answers, I can lay him to rest…in my mind."

"What answers would they be, son?" Harry asked, and watched Gabriel take another healthy gulp.

"What—what was he like, my dad? I mean, as a friend. When he was *your* friend," he added, pointing a finger towards each of them.

The question forced them to think of the man they'd killed, and it made them uncomfortable.

"He was…" Arthur sipped his drink and tried again, searching for the right words. "He was… a good man. A better man than any of us."

They couldn't argue with that, but it wasn't something they chose to remember.

"He was a drunk," Gabriel muttered, and raised his glass as if to toast himself. "Looks like I'm going in the same direction, eh?"

"You're amongst friends, Gabe," Harry crooned. "No need to worry when you're with people you can trust. Enjoy yourself."

"Y'know, this morning, I found a load of empty bottles in my kitchen," Gabriel told them, crooking a finger so they'd lean in to hear the details. "I don't know how they got there, but it must've been me who drank them all, mustn't it? It can't have been my dad…"

He trailed off, as if questioning his own sanity.

"Living at Wharf House isn't good for you," Derek said, and gave him an awkward pat on the back. "Why don't you listen to your Uncle Derek, eh? Go back to that lovely place in Charlestown, and get back to your old life. Being here, surrounded by memories, isn't doing you any good at all."

"I can't go back now," Gabriel muttered, and threw back the rest of his drink, much to their amazement. "When I'm here, at the old house, I feel close to him again."

"I worry for you, Gabe," Tom said. "If you carry on the way you are, there's every chance you'll end up on the same path John did, and with the same end. We'd hate to see that happen, wouldn't we?"

They all nodded.

"Some days, I wonder if it would be better," Gabriel said, drunkenly. "At least, then, we'd be together again, and with my mum, too."

An afterlife wasn't something he believed in, but they weren't to know that. Just as they weren't to know that every drop of 'gin' he'd imbibed that evening had the chemical formula H_2O.

"I can't—can't believe he's gone—"

"Come on, lad, I think it's time you went home, don't you?"

Gabriel shook his head, but allowed them to help him up and out of his chair. Behind his back, Harry made a universal sign to indicate he'd had too much to the barman, and for the benefit of any of the other punters at the bar.

It was already late, almost midnight, and the night air was beginning to pick up with the beginnings of a storm.

"I need to walk this off," Gabriel said. "Get some fresh air. That's what I need to do."

The others checked the vicinity, looked at each other and then, finally, to Harry, who was the final arbiter when it came to matters such as these. After all, he would be in charge of the eventual cover-up, so he had the privilege of making the final call.

"Yes, that's a good idea," he said, having satisfied himself there were no other people within range to see them. Although it was the centre of town, its residents were mostly at home, there being no live music on that night and the restaurants and most of the bars being on the other side of the harbour.

"This—this way," Gabriel said, and tripped over his toes on the cobblestones.

"Mind your step," Harry said. "We wouldn't want you to fall."

Derek laughed beneath his breath, and smiled broadly as they passed Wharf House, which he could safely say would very soon be his.

"Along here," Gabriel said, leading them towards Smeaton's Pier. "This is where it happened, isn't it? Where he fell."

They said nothing, but continued to walk beside him, circling like vultures in human form.

They watched the younger man weave his way along the pier, stumbling here and there, and remembered that, with John, they'd been forced to immobilise the man first, and dump his body over the side of the pier afterwards. His son had the good grace to save them the hassle by walking towards his own place of execution without any fuss at all.

He always was a good lad.

"This is the spot," Gabriel said, coming to the particular place in the stonework, which he knew like the back of his hand. "They found him down there."

He tipped forward to look and, for a second, they thought he was a goner.

He reared back again, and Derek let out a disappointed *hiss* between his teeth.

Gabriel turned to face them all, still looking disoriented, with very little command of his faculties or his limbs.

"I know it was one of you," he said, and watched each man's face register a degree of calculated shock. "I don't care anymore. I just want to be with him again, that's all. Before I go, I want to know. Put me out of my misery. Tell me which—which one of you it was."

He stumbled again, almost losing his footing over the edge of the pier.

The four other men looked amongst themselves, and Tom gave a firm shake of his head and made a slicing motion with his hand over his throat, but Harry overruled it and decided that it was only fair that a man had a final request. It seemed fitting.

"What are you talking about, Gabe? You're making no sense."

"I know, that's what I'm trying to tell you. I *know* it was one of you. I remember the argument, and in my dreams I remember that the voice belonged to one of you, but I can't remember which one. I just need to know, before it's over. As a favour to your old friend, before you shove me off the edge, too." He leaned forward and braced his hands on his knees, as if he could no longer stand upright.

"He's a mess," Arthur muttered, and Harry held up an imperious hand.

"Where's Sophie tonight, Gabriel? I thought you were growing close."

"She's nothing special," came the reply. "Just a bit of fun, to try to distract myself. Isn't working anymore, so what's the point? I told her to go away. Go home."

They were satisfied with that.

"You can't really believe one of us was involved in John's death," Arthur said, but Gabriel nodded his head vehemently.

"I think it was the smuggling," he said. "He must've found out, and that's why you pushed him, isn't it?"

"What do you know about smuggling, Gabe?"

"I think it's where my idea for *Ethan's Adventures* subconsciously came from," he replied. "You four are the Mystery Men, aren't you?"

He began to laugh, as if he'd told the funniest joke in the world.

"I thought it was my imagination, but it wasn't. On some level, I've always known why you killed him, and it must've leaked out in my stories. I reckon you've probably got some barrels out there even now, hidden underwater, haven't you?"

They said nothing, but continued to watch him with their snake eyes.

"C'mon," he mumbled. "Tell me which one of you it was. You owe me that."

"We owe you nothing," Derek snapped, but a single look from Tom and Harry had him buttoning up again.

"Let's say you're right, Gabe," Harry said. "Let's say one of us killed your dad. Does it matter which one it was?"

Gabriel could sense the revelation coming, and told himself to stay focused and stay in character.

They were so close.

"I just need to know," he repeated. "So I can leave knowing the truth."

Harry shrugged, and stuck his hands in his trousers. "You won't be leaving this pier,

Gabriel. There's only one way out for you, now. Do you understand that? You can't continue to threaten our organisation, like your dad did—like Gallagher did. There's too much at stake."

Gabriel rubbed a hand over his eyes, and acted like a man who was finding it hard to remain upright.

"I under—understand."

They took a collective step forward, forcing him to take an involuntary step backward towards the edge. Around them, a heavy sea fret began to roll in, wrapping itself around the five lone men who braved the elements.

"I suppose there's no harm, now," Harry said, and turned to look at the man who'd sent John Rowe into his next life.

"I had to do it, Gabriel. He left me no choice," Arthur said. "I didn't *want* to. I *had* to."

"Wh—what for? The smuggling?"

"Yes," Arthur said. "We invited him to be a part of it from the beginning. He had the chance, but he turned it down. He looked the other way for a while, but then, he couldn't keep his mouth shut. His drinking was getting worse, and he was talking about anything and everything. It was only a matter of time."

Arthur shook his head, sadly. "In some ways, maybe it was a kindness."

Gabriel saw red, then. His anger was an inferno, blazing through his body and burning its way through the dramatic performance of his life.

Harry saw the change, and held up a hand. "Wait—he's—" He looked closely into Gabriel's eyes, and swore. "He's faking the whole bloody thing."

Harry lunged forward, and made a grab for him.

Listening at the other end of the wire Gabriel wore on his chest, Sophie and a field operative from the Ghost Squad snatched up their mics and gave the command for all units to enter, which they did—like lightning. They descended on the pier with sirens blaring, blue flashing lights and powerful spotlights that cut through the night air to illuminate the four older men who searched this way and that for a way out of their predicament, like mice scurrying inside a cage.

As several running figures approached at speed, Harry turned to the others, then to his godson.

"Jenna was sorry about the banana bread," he said.

Gabriel smiled like a shark through the mist. "You can tell her, if you ever see one another again, that her cake was dry."

On which parting note, he began walking back to Wharf House, which no longer bore the same sadness for him as before. At the end of the pier, a slim, dark-haired woman waited for him, and suddenly he found he was no longer walking but running, headlong and with open arms, towards a bright new future.

EPILOGUE

Six months later

Ethan felt the rain against his cheeks, biting and cold as it had been on the night his father went missing. But, this time, he didn't mind it so much, because he knew that behind every storm the sunshine awaited, bright and bold, just as he was. He was so close to finding the Mystery Men, now, and he had the coordinates for their hideout...

"Mr Rowe?"

Gabriel looked up from reading a paragraph of his new book to seek out the source of the interruption. There was a sea of children's faces sitting cross-legged on the floor of the St Ives

Public Library, which would have been enough to strike terror into his girlfriend's heart. As Sophie had often told him, she'd sooner face a ruthless criminal in a darkened alley than an audience of pre-teenage kids, because the criminals were far less brutal.

"Mr Rowe, where did Ethan find the coordinates?"

"I was just coming to that," he said, tapping the book he held. "It turns out that he finds them on the back of a painting."

"Who painted the painting?"

"If you just listen, you'll find out—"

"Where did the painting come from?"

"It'll all become clear—"

"What if the coordinates are wrong?"

"They're not wrong."

"What about Mystery Women? My mummy says we should be equal in all things."

"It's just a collective term I used to describe members of the smuggling gang regardless of gender. However, if it makes her feel better, your mummy can be a baddie in my next book—there, problem solved!" he said, feeling a bit harassed.

"Mr Rowe, my mummy asked me to ask you whether you're married."

"Not yet," he said. "But I've met the woman I'm hoping to marry, if she'll have me."

"What if she doesn't believe in marriage?"

"Then we'll live in sin."

"What's sin?"

"Ask your dad."

"Mr Rowe? Where do babies come from?"

"Weekend mini-breaks, as far as I can tell."

"What's your wife like?"

"She isn't my wife yet, and you can't go spoiling the surprise. She's the kindest, strongest person I've ever known, and I love her."

"She loves you, too," Sophie whispered, from the back of the room, before slipping out again to meet Turner, who was studying for his detective's exam, on her recommendation.

As for her, she was no longer a sergeant, but an inspector.

As she made her way towards the station, she whistled an old tune from long ago, one her father had often sung and which, for many years, she'd avoided. Now, with him laid to rest at Barnoon Cemetery along with all the other ghosts, she allowed herself to sing proudly about her boat coming in.

AUTHOR'S NOTE

St Ives is one of my favourite places in the world, and we've spent many happy times on the beaches around the bay area with our two children. For that reason, it was an intimidating task to consider writing a story set around an area I hold so dear…but then, I reminded myself that, over the past ten years, I must have killed off at least half of the fictional population of Northumberland in my DCI Ryan novels, so it was past time that Cornwall was treated to a bit of the same medicine! Unlike the Ryan books or my Dr Gregory thrillers, these Summer Suspense books are intended to be lighter reads with a smattering of romance and suspense, rather than the heavier crime thriller content you might find in some of my other novels.

Now, for a word on real-life businesses and locations. Wherever I have used the real name of a place, such as The Sloop, rest assured it is because I think very highly of it, and harbour no intention to malign the place or its people. Remember, folks, it's always only fiction, and wherever you turn in a town like St Ives, you will find some new little nook or cranny with an artisan coffee shop, an ice-cream counter or pottery counter to be explored, which is something I would encourage if you ever have the opportunity to visit.

The St Ives Bookseller is a real place, and a lovely one, at that. It's small but perfectly formed, and having signed books there myself, as well as at the St Ives Library, I could easily imagine my character Gabriel surrounded by books and a warm welcome from the staff at both, and for that I am very grateful!

Finally, to my readers, thank you again for making *The Bay* a #1 bestseller in the

United Kingdom. I am always overwhelmed by your support of my work, and I truly hope you enjoy the story.

Until next time…

LJ ROSS
AUGUST 2023

ABOUT THE AUTHOR

LJ Ross is an international bestselling author, best known for creating atmospheric mystery and thriller novels, including the DCI Ryan series of Northumbrian murder mysteries which have sold over seven million copies worldwide.

Her debut, *Holy Island,* was released in January 2015 and reached number one in the UK and Australian charts. Since then, she has released more than twenty further novels, all of which have been top three global bestsellers and almost all of which have been UK #1 bestsellers. Louise has garnered an army of loyal readers through her storytelling and, thanks to them, many of her books reached the coveted #1 spot whilst only available to pre-order ahead of release.

Louise was born in Northumberland, England. She studied undergraduate and postgraduate Law at King's College, University of London and then abroad in Paris and Florence. She spent much of her working life in London, where she was a lawyer for a number of years until taking the decision to change career and pursue her dream to write. Now, she writes full time and lives with her family in Northumberland. She enjoys reading all manner of books, travelling and spending time with family and friends.

If you enjoyed *The Bay,* please consider leaving a review online.

If you would like to be kept up to date with new releases from LJ Ross, please complete an e-mail contact form on her Facebook page or website, www.ljrossauthor.com

Scan the QR code below to find out
more about LJ Ross and her books

If you'd like to discover Gabrielle
and Luke's story, check out

THE COVE

A SUMMER SUSPENSE MYSTERY (BOOK #1)

THE PERFECT ESCAPE...

Gabrielle Adams has it all – brains, beauty, a
handsome fiancé, and a dream job in publishing.
Until, one day, everything changes.

The 'Underground Killer' takes his victims when they
least expect it: standing on the edge of a busy Tube
platform, as they wait for a train to arrive through
the murky underground tunnels of London.

Gabrielle soon learns that being a survivor is harder
than being a victim, and she struggles to return to
her old life. Desperate to break free from the endless
nightmares, she snatches up an opportunity to run a tiny
bookshop in a picturesque cove in rural Cornwall.

She thinks she's found the perfect escape, but has
she swapped one nightmare for another?

Suspense and mystery are peppered with romance
and humour in this fast-paced thriller, set amidst
the spectacular Cornish landscape.

If you'd like to discover Kate and
Nick's story, check out

THE CREEK

A SUMMER SUSPENSE MYSTERY (BOOK #2)

YOU CAN RUN, BUT YOU CAN'T HIDE...

Kate Irving arrives at her grandfather's cottage at Frenchman's
Creek in the dead of night with her young son, a small
suitcase and little else. Its scattered community of fishermen,
farmers, artists and jetsetters barely bat an eyelid, because
theirs is a rarefied world, tucked beneath the lush forest that
lines the banks of the Helford Estuary, deep in the heart
of Cornwall, where life is slow and people generally mind
their own business. Unless, of course, your grandfather
happens to be a pillar of the local community...

Kate's left the past behind and guards her privacy and her
son fiercely. She's wary of accepting the friendship her new
neighbours offer, but their kindness is too great to refuse and she
begins to feel she has found her place in the world. That is, until
tragedy strikes, and her new friends look to her for the answers...

Kate soon learns that the past always catches up with you, in the
end—the question is, will she be able to face it, when it does?

If you enjoyed *The Bay*, why not try the
bestselling DCI Ryan Mysteries by LJ Ross?

HOLY ISLAND

A DCI RYAN MYSTERY (Book #1)

Detective Chief Inspector Ryan retreats to Holy Island seeking sanctuary when he is forced to take sabbatical leave from his duties as a homicide detective. A few days before Christmas, his peace is shattered, and he is thrust back into the murky world of murder when a young woman is found dead amongst the ancient ruins of the nearby Priory.

When former local girl Dr Anna Taylor arrives back on the island as a police consultant, old memories swim to the surface making her confront her difficult past. She and Ryan struggle to work together to hunt a killer who hides in plain sight, while pagan ritual and small-town politics muddy the waters of their investigation.

Murder and mystery are peppered with a sprinkling of romance and humour in this fast-paced crime whodunnit set on the spectacular Northumbrian island of Lindisfarne, cut off from the English mainland by a tidal causeway.

If you like the Summer Suspense Mysteries, why not try
the bestselling Alexander Gregory Thrillers by LJ Ross?

IMPOSTOR

AN ALEXANDER GREGORY THRILLER (Book #1)

There's a killer inside all of us...

After an elite criminal profiling unit is shut down amidst
a storm of scandal and mismanagement, only one
person emerges unscathed. Forensic psychologist Doctor
Alexander Gregory has a reputation for being able to step
inside the darkest minds to uncover whatever secrets lie
hidden there and, soon enough, he finds himself drawn
into the murky world of murder investigation.

In the beautiful hills of County Mayo, Ireland, a killer is on
the loose. Panic has a stranglehold on its rural community
and the Garda are running out of time. Gregory has
sworn to follow a quiet life but, when the call comes, can
he refuse to help their desperate search for justice?

Murder and mystery are peppered with dark humour in this
fast-paced thriller set amidst the spectacular Irish landscape.

IMPOSTOR is available now in all good bookshops!

LOVE READING?

JOIN THE CLUB...

Join the LJ Ross Book Club to connect with a thriving community of fellow book lovers! To receive a free monthly newsletter with exclusive author interviews and giveaways, sign up at www.ljrossauthor.com or follow the LJ Ross Book Club on social media:

 #LJBookClubTweet

 @LJRossAuthor

 @ljrossauthor

Made in the USA
Middletown, DE
28 November 2023

43895203R00229